Why She Chose Life

Sarah Roberts Smith

Scott Rocha • Canada

2020 Digital Edition
ISBN 978-1-7772849-4-7
2020 Paperback Edition
ISBN 978-1-7772849-3-0

For my family, friends and loved ones. Without you all, I don't know where I would be today. Thank you for everything. I love you

Author's note

To this day, I still have nightmares of the torment. Nightmares of being trapped with no way out. The abuse doesn't end once you leave. It leaves its scars, and it leaves subtle reminders that there was a time that you weren't okay and constantly suffering. I'm here to tell you that it gets better, it will, but it does take its toll on your entire life.

This book was inspired by true events. Many of the events, things said, and things done, happened to me during my seven-year abusive relationship. I didn't realize that it was abusive until I was so far in it that it was hard to get out. I had people try to warn me but, I couldn't see what they saw. I had seen some things that made me question our relationship, but I just made excuses for you.

This book started as diary entries. I wanted to share my experience in hopes of shedding light on domestic abuse, sharing the raw parts of it, and spreading awareness. I also wanted to share my story so that others know they are not alone or crazy. I wanted to share because this is the reality that we are told to hush and keep quiet about. We are too scared to speak up because when we do, we are called liars, told it's not that bad, and asked if he's that horrible to you, why don't you leave? I too asked this question before I was in that situation. I didn't know that it is not just as easy as leaving and that just because you do leave, does not mean the abuse will stop. These people are narcissistic, manipulative, sociopaths...psychopaths. I did a report in university on Charles Manson; it terrified me when I did research on him because I realized how much he sounded like my ex-partner.

This is the reality for so many women. They keep quiet. They live in fear. I lived in fear. If my story can reach even one person, validate their feelings and emotions, help them to know they are not crazy, give them the courage to leave, or bring awareness to something so common in today's society, then it was worth it to share something I held in for over seven years.

There are many things in this book that might be hard to read, but this was my reality. I was being mentally and psychologically tortured. I tried to convey that torture and pain the best that I could, but I don't think the torment I felt could ever fully be put into words. I am leaving abuse hotline numbers on the back pages of this book. I know it's incredibly hard. I know it seems dim and like there's no way out, but you are worthy. You deserve the world and more. Their words do not define you. Hold onto that hope and to that fire within you. Don't let them snuff out that flame. There's help and there's support available. You are strong and you are amazing. Don't forget that. Ever

1.

I was trapped and your demons had become my own. There was no escaping the evil that had taken over. I was being held hostage within my darkest thoughts. The thoughts that had consumed my entire being. The darkness that had taken over and buried the light that used to shine so bright. When the thoughts came out to play, they would scream at me all hours of the night. You are worthless, nothing but a waste of life, no matter what you do, it will never be good enough, it doesn't matter how hard you fucking try, it will never matter, everything that has happened to you, everything you have been through, is completely your fault. You are the problem. You will never matter. I tried to drown out these demons and take control back, but I was weak, and these thoughts just kept screaming louder and louder and, with every day spent with you, it became harder and harder to fight them off.

I truly believed that you loved me, and I loved you. I couldn't understand why the pain wouldn't just stop, why you couldn't just love me, why I couldn't love myself. Why wasn't I enough? If I could just be better, maybe things wouldn't have got to this point. Maybe things wouldn't be so bad if I were just fucking better.

2.

It was 12:00 a.m., I sat on the cold tiles of my bathroom floor, and the house was silent. All that I heard was the sound of the bathtub faucet slowly dripping and the sound of subtle weeping as blackened tears rolled down my cheeks. In my hand, I held a large, serrated knife. Gripping the handle tightly, I took the cold metal blade and placed it against my left wrist. My flesh hugged the blade. My skin now shared the sharp coolness the blade had to offer. With force, I pushed down on the blade and pulled towards my body, feeling each bump of metal through my opening flesh as my fist clenched in defence from the burning and tearing sensation. My hand that held the knife dropped to my side as I lifted my other arm above my head. I then watched the thick, dark, red blood roll down my arm and into the cubital fossa. For a moment, the blood pooled there until it could hold no more and began dripping down the sides of my elbow and onto the tile where I sat. I no longer felt tense. The emotional pain I felt just minutes ago, had faded away. I had fed into my dark thoughts, given them what they wanted— the satisfaction and the release they begged for. At this moment, despite the burning from the fresh wound that lay diagonally on my left wrist, I felt okay. I took comfort in the burning sensation. I took comfort in the fact that what I had just done was ultimately my decision. Screaming thoughts or not, I took this knife, and I made the decision to slide it across my wrist and open myself up. It was me who controlled this pain I was now feeling, not you. Although, in the very back of my mind, even though I felt in control and I made this decision to cope with the emotional pain you inflicted on me, it was as if you were sitting right there behind me. Your chest to my back, arms wrapped around me, your hand on mine, guiding my hand, guiding the blade. But no, I sat on the bathroom floor, back against the wall, alone.

3.

November 2, 2016 was the day I had lost hope. I felt like I had been fighting a losing battle and no matter how hard I tried, I would fail. Even though cutting took away the emotional pain, even though I felt okay in the moments after, I also felt this immense empty feeling deep inside my chest. I couldn't live like this anymore; the pain on a good day was almost unbearable. There was nothing but struggle like I was lost at sea trying to swim against the current, battling the waves, not a boat or island in sight. Hope became more of a dream than a reality. What was I fighting for? Where was I going? Taking a blade to my wrist was a temporary fix. It wouldn't be enough for long as the relief would soon be filled with the urge to cut again, like an addiction. You say just one more fix but that urge always comes back, and soon you lose all control. Was I really in control? Or was it a matter of it controlling me? Was I in control when I chose to give in to the urge, I had coursing through my body, that itch on my wrist telling me what I had to do?

On this day, I truly considered ending my life. I wanted to put an end to the immense empty feeling within my chest, the unbearable pain, and the dark thoughts marinating my brain. I thought that if I took the blade, cut a little deeper and laid down to sleep, everything would stop. It was at this moment, that I realized how bad things really were. I wanted to give up. The girl who fought through anything, the girl who always looked on the bright side no matter how grim the situation, the girl who lived on hope, had finally brought out that white flag and violently waved it around begging for mercy. I surrendered my entire being and everything that I had been or ever was. I thought I had lost all hope. I felt dead inside, and that realization was like a shock to the heart. This was what brought me back and when I took that first long deep breath in after the shock, it was like breathing new life. I replayed certain events in my head, the events that brought me to where I am today, the ones that contributed to me almost ending my life and the decision to fight back and live. I had realized I couldn't give up, that that was not an option, and there was still fight left in me. I recognized how much I had to fight for and what it was I had to do to save myself.

4.

I remember the events of 2010 very clearly. I was a young Mom to a silly and smart two-year-old, exploring the exciting world of single parenting and life. I had separated from my ex-partner just three months earlier. We had been high school sweethearts. We began dating in grade nine and ended up having Greyson at the beginning of grade 12. While I was raising Greyson and trying to graduate on time, my partner was still living his teen life. He was around but not as much as he should have been, and his mother wasn't exactly encouraging him to be a father. Miraculously, we both graduated with our class and then I took the year off to raise Greyson. I had planned to go to college after I figured out what I wanted to do in life. That summer, we were together on and off and I knew it wasn't going to last but didn't want to be another teenage statistic. We fought often enough that we thought it was best to just end it.

Adjusting to single life and being a full-time, single mother was different, but it was amazing. It was all about Greyson and I at that time and I was completely okay with that. There was a part of me that wished and longed for a love life like in the movies, but I was content.

Soon after the break-up, my friends invited me to go dancing at a club called Matt and Joe's. This was only my second or third time going there because I didn't get out much after having Greyson. I was excited to have a girls' night on the town with Stephanie and Carly. I remember this day so damn vividly because this was the day that changed my life. The day that I had made a simple decision to go dancing with friends, all the while not knowing the huge impact it would have on my life. That one little decision that will forever be a part of me and the one I cannot take back. This was the day we had met.

I can feel the cold on my skin when I think of standing in the lineup at Matt and Joe's that night. We waited to get out of the chill of the night and into the warmth of the night club. Stephanie, Carly, and I were giggling and laughing as we huddled together to try and stay warm. We were also trying to keep our composure as we were already tipsy from the 26er we had split at Stephanie's. We would pre-drink before going out to save some money and it was always fun to have a little to drink while we did up our makeup and tried on 10 different outfits. until we found the perfect one.

Looking back, I realize that my outfit of the night was a poor choice considering the weather, but there I stood in a skirt and heels with a shirt that showed quite a bit of cleavage.

My legs had been freezing but my cheeks felt hot and my throat numb with a pleasant buzz. We waited in line behind five other people, people who had dressed appropriately for the weather. Once in the club, we left our jackets in the coat check. We walked past the bar and shimmied our way through the crowd of people to get to the dance floor. We were swaying our hips as we stumbled about, the alcohol really taking effect. Something about the pink and blue lights mixed with the music and movement of our bodies really amped up the buzz. It took about 10-15 minutes of dancing before a man approached our little group. He came in smiling and dancing beside Carly. We welcomed him in to dance with us. It took a moment before I got a good look at him, but when I did, he looked familiar. I danced closer to him, placed my hand on his shoulder, and pulled him a little closer to me to ask him a question. I asked him if we knew each other. He responded with a question directed at all of us.

"Do you remember a bald chubby guy the last time you guys were here?"

We all gasped overly dramatically, adding in a sincere, "oh my gosh!" and "that was you?"

His name was Derrick, we danced with him the last time we had our ladies' night a few months back. Wow, did he look different! He had slimmed down quite a bit, I'd say he had lost about 30 pounds, and he no longer rocked the bald look. Instead, he had a full head of thick, dark hair. He looked like a completely different person.

We danced for a few more minutes until Derrick asked if his two buddies could join us. He reassured us that they were great guys and a lot of fun. Feeling tipsy and silly, I was the first to pipe up and tell him to bring them on over. He waved them over from a corner table near the dance floor. Two tall men headed towards us. One wearing a black T-shirt with short blonde hair and the other wearing a red shirt with black designs with dark brown hair. Both carrying a Canadian in one hand.

The guy with dark brown hair walked right up to me and shook my hand. That dark-haired man was you. Your words were smooth and very charming. We danced and talked long after last-call and closed down the bar. When we finally had to part, we exchanged numbers. I remember the last words you spoke to me that night. As you smiled you said to me, "Can't wait to hear from you Victoria, have a great night." Then you were gone. This was the beginning; this is how it all started. I find it slightly amusing now, not funny but in a dark sense, how this thought used to be happy and a cute story of how we met. When I look back at the memory now, I think to myself how stupid I was to meet a boy in a bar. I wish I could say this memory was filled with regret, but I don't regret having my children with you. I can say that this memory is filled with pain and that instead of being the beginning of a love story, it was the beginning of a never-ending nightmare, the beginning of a horror novel.

5.

After meeting that night, we talked every day. We got together after three weeks of talking and you ended up meeting Greyson right away. You brought him a toy car and we spent the day at the park. You were great with Greyson, it made me happy to see his little smiles and you running after him while playing tag. We continued talking and I felt like we had this special connection. We shared fears and dreams and talked about anything and everything.

About two months after that meeting at the park, the girls and I had another night out. We all met up at the bar and ended up staying the night at your apartment. We had kissed before this, but we had yet to have sex. It was a bit nerve-wracking to think about having sex with someone other than Greyson's Dad since he had been my one and only. I think the vodka we had drunk before gave me that push, that courage to take that next step. I didn't feel pressured into it. It was something I did want to experience with you, but it wasn't something I would normally do so early in a relationship. Our first time wasn't something you would remember for being romantic or amazing, more of a did we really just have our first time on a bathroom floor type thing. After we had sex, the perfect first time or not, I felt more of a connection with you. I was old school in a lot of my beliefs and sex wasn't just sex to me, it meant more. You were sharing your body with someone and you and that person were making a special connection, one that you wouldn't make with many others. So, in my head, I thought regardless of how or where it was, it was special. Later, I found that you didn't have the same beliefs, that sex really wasn't anything to you other than just sex. Two people pleasing each other and that was it. Then later to discover that it was more about you being pleasured and not caring about the other person. That wasn't pure selfishness, that was more about your view on women and how they should be treated compared to how they should treat you.

6.

Rapid knocking on the bathroom door pulled me from my thoughts. I shuffled in a panic around the bathroom floor, slipping on my blood, spreading it more on the white tile. "Fuck, Fuck, Fuck," I thought as I tried to quickly find a towel and clean up the mess on the floor. I stood up. "Just a minute." I hid the knife under the sink, behind the cleaner. I pulled my shirt sleeve down to cover my wrist and grabbed the black towel hanging from behind the door. I could hear your impatient sighs from the hallway. Once I finished wiping up the blood, I threw the towel in the hamper and stood in front of the mirror. I wiped the dried black tears from my face and fixed my hair into a bun. I then turned to face the door and took a deep breath in before grabbing the handle and turning it to the right until I heard a little click. The cooled air from the hallway rushed into the bathroom as the door opened, giving me goosebumps all over my body, and seeing you standing there looking exasperated, sent a shiver down my spine. "I'm sorry, I was just using the washroom." You said nothing as you forced your way through, shoving me over with your shoulder in the process. I lost my balance and fell into the door. You grabbed the doorknob and demanded I leave. I stood back up and headed towards the stairway. Barely making it out of the doorway, the door slammed shut behind me. I could hear the shower curtain open, the dripping bathtub faucet becoming a full flow of water, and then the click of the shower. I felt relieved because I knew you would be at least 45 minutes in the shower. You were angry about our argument earlier when I had tried to sit down after I got the kids to bed. There were things that needed to be done around the house, but I just wanted to get in some ink time.

Speaking never really came easily for me. I would always trip up on my words and forget things I wanted to say, especially when I was upset or angry. I just couldn't get the words out of my mouth when speaking. Writing came to me naturally. It flowed with no hesitation and no second-guessing. I could just pick up a pen and start writing. It had been a while since I was able to sit down and actually get in some writing. I had thought about it all day and I had all these ideas swimming through my brain that I needed to get out. Once I sat down to write, there were soft yet rapid footsteps that came down to the living room. Knowing who it was, I stayed focused on my notebook. Low mumbling broke the silence in the quiet room. I couldn't hear exactly what you were saying as you walked past me, but I could take a pretty good guess it was a complaint. You took a seat on the other end of the couch. I continued to write as you shuffled through your bag, pulling out your laptop, cell phone, and TV remote that you had locked in your bag whenever you weren't using them. The TV turned on. The volume was turned up to a very distracting level as the announcer shouted about a missed goal. Then you spoke up in a very condescending tone. "How about you put your crap away and actually watch the game with me?" Right then and there, I knew this would turn into something. I really didn't care for hockey and didn't get a chance to do my writing very often. It always irritated me that you were never supportive of my writing and regularly called it crap. I didn't stop writing but I did respond to you. I told you I would pay attention and watch it with you in a bit because I really wanted to get some ink time in and was kind of on a roll. As usual, you weren't pleased with my answer. You wanted me to put my things away and say yes with a smile on my face.

You snapped back with, "This is why we could never work; you are selfish and too consumed by your shit." And, of course, you weren't done after that. You had to firmly place the TV remote in the middle of the couch and continue. "You are never interested in anything I like; it's been a fucking struggle the entire relationship."

Knowing that this was going to get more heated, I tried keeping my voice gentle and low. "Listen, I don't want this to turn into an argument, all I wanted was to-" and before getting a full sentence out, you stopped me.

"Maybe it wouldn't be an argument, Victoria, if you put the fucking effort into someone other than yourself. What are you even writing about? How much you hate me? What a piece of shit I am? What are you writing about that's so important?"

At this point, I felt irritated and annoyed. All I wanted to do was write. So I responded with, "You know I am writing a book." Well, you had a field day with that one.

"Is Victoria writing a book? Top fucking seller? Get your thick fucking head out of the clouds, it's not realistic, you're wasting your time on nothing but shit. Do you really think that you will follow through with it and finish it? There are hundreds of authors out there and you aren't one of them!" he yelled.

At this point, it was getting hard to hide my frustration. A huge lump grew in my throat. Looking down at my page, half-filled with words, half a blank paper waiting for the words stuck in my head, I knew I would be going to bed tonight with this page half empty. I spoke up, which you didn't like. "We all have hobbies and things that we enjoy. You like hockey and your computer; I like reading and writing. I don't usually put myself first and I have really tried with you. I watch your shows and I discuss things that you are interested in. Why can't I just write for a little bit? I don't say what you like is a waste of time. I enjoy writing, it makes me happy. I just got the kids to sleep and it's been a long day, so I..." Then I was cut off again and you were angry.

The condescending tone had never left your voice, but there was anger mixed in with it now. "Yeah, Victoria, you just got the kids to sleep and decided to completely ignore all your responsibilities and sit on your ass and write nonsense. There are dishes that are sitting in the sink that need to be washed, the living room is a fucking pig stye, and laundry needs to be done. I told you earlier that I needed some laundry done. I get that you don't give a shit about the state of the house you live in, but I do."

I never knew what to say to you in these moments. I felt like it was always a situation where I was damned if I did and damned if I didn't. I looked down at my page, I didn't know what to say but I knew what to write and that's all I wanted to do. Then a sharp pain pulled my eyes from the page and to you as a toy fell onto my lap.

"You fucking show me the respect I damn well deserve and look me in the fucking eyes when I am speaking to you," he yelled. I fought back tears, knowing that seeing me cry would only add fuel to the fire. I didn't know how to respond back without you completely losing it on me. I used my silence as a defence. Which didn't stop you from continuing anyways. "You know what Victoria, maybe I wouldn't have to do shit like that if you had some basic human mannerisms," he continued.

This made my blood boil. I was so sick of you giving excuses to throw things at me or hit me. So, I broke my silence and again spoke up. "It still doesn't give you the right to throw something at me. I told you I didn't want to fight. I had been cleaning all day and taking care of the kids. Yes, there are a few small things that need to be done around the house, but I was going to take care of it after I was able to get in some time for myself. You could help me out a little bit with some of the cleaning as well. We could work together so that we both can have time to ourselves and time to relax. Writing winds me down and I don't do it often."

You chuckled and began mocking me again. "Oh, I'm tired. I did this and that all day long. I couldn't sit on my fat ass all day because I have responsibilities. That's the answer, Victoria. I'll just do everything for you and that will solve everything! Or, now hear me out on this one, make sure you're actually fucking listening. You could learn how to delegate your time better so that you could get it done. You can't depend on other people to do shit for you. It's adulthood, so grow the fuck up."

I had no words left to say, only tears that had been trying to get out and couldn't be held back anymore.

"Oh, here it comes!" You raised your arms, waving them around as if calling people over. "Everyone gather around for Victoria's pity party! She can't handle the truth or adulthood, someone come save her! She needs saving, so who's it going to be? Come rescue the whiny, lazy bitch."

After that, I picked up my notebook and placed it under my arm. My chest felt like fire and my eyes were stinging with each tear that fell. I stood up and grabbed my lukewarm tea from the coffee table. I looked at you and kept my voice low and calm, when all I wanted to do was yell and scream. "I said I didn't want to fight. I'm going to bed."

You sat back in your seat and opened up your laptop. "Yeah, okay, run away again. You can't handle an adult conversation, as usual. Thanks for watching the game with me and making me look like an asshole because you can't act your fucking age. And you wonder why our relationship failed."

I tried to bite my tongue. I really did. "This is not an adult conversation. You always have to belittle me. I don't want to sit here and argue or defend myself while you call me names because I didn't do what you wanted me to when you wanted me to do it. I am always the damn problem. I know, alright, I get it." I tried not to have my attitude show in my voice, but I couldn't help it. I couldn't stop myself from adding in a mocking tone when I said I was the problem.

You snapped back quickly. "Yeah, actually you are the problem and you fucking know it."

I wiped the tears from my face with my sleeve and nodded my head in agreeance before turning and walking up the stairs. I placed my tea on the kitchen table and made my way up to the room, checking in on the boys on the way up. My notebook and pen were placed on my desk and I laid in bed. The hockey game was loud downstairs. I laid on my back in the dark and empty bedroom we had shared for the last few years. I looked up at the ceiling fan, slowly turning. Dark thoughts and feelings were consuming me. I had decided to get up and take a bath and to release some of the pain that had been overwhelming my heart. Before long, it was 12:00a.m and now, here I am standing on the stairs, lost in thought.

7.

I was relieved that you decided to have a shower, while it interrupted what I had been doing, I knew you would be occupied for the next 45 minutes or so and then retreat to bed. This gave me a break from arguing, this gave me time to reflect and figure out what the hell I was going to do.

As I made my way down to the living room, I checked the boys again. Watching their little chests move up and down as they slept peacefully, gave me comfort. It put my mind at ease that my babies were all safe. Although they were all past the age of worrying about SIDS, I could never shake the fear. I continued back down to the living room and flopped myself down on the couch. Closing my eyes, I could hear the water from the shower, hitting the curtain and splashing off the walls.

What the fuck am I going to do? I sat, hands on my head, gripping my hair, and repeated this over and over. Getting away was the only option at this point. Figuring out how was difficult. You always used scare tactics, so that in the end, it always looked like it was my decision to stay. Every time I made that decision, there would be follow up conversations on how much you loved me and if you didn't, you wouldn't be here. Then you would go over everything that I had to work on and fix about myself in order to save the relationship. I hear your voice in my head, all day and night. I remember the sinking feeling in my gut every time I heard the lecture after I chose to stay. I remember how I offered other solutions or gave my opinion and how it was always shut down. I was told to shut up and do as you say. You were always the more intelligent one in the relationship. I was nothing compared to you. I was lucky to have you.

I knew that we could never work as a team because nothing I ever did was good enough. I couldn't stay this time. It never got any better. After the first time you became physical, I knew it would only get worse from there. There was no turning back at that point. This wasn't about me having to fix myself and it never was. This was about my children and what I had to do for them. They couldn't live like this anymore. They weren't allowed to be children and they couldn't like anything you didn't like. They too walked on eggshells just like I did, but for them, it was much worse. I couldn't take watching them grow up like this; it hurt me. Keeping a family together isn't always what's most important, not in this situation anyway. Having Mommy and Daddy together wasn't what was best for these boys. I wasn't staying for them, I was staying out of fear. Fear was what kept me here, but I had to overcome that fear and I needed to make a decision to leave for good. I just didn't know at the time how the fuck I was going to do it.

8.

The thought of our first argument came to mind. The first argument that should have ended our relationship. It was after New Year's Eve and by that time, we had been seeing each other since October. You spent most of your weekends at the bar and I had decided to tag along one night. When we had arrived, two women approached us in line. They immediately jumped all over you in excitement. They bombarded you with questions, asking how you had been, where you were living now, and asked if they would be seeing you on the dance floor. I was pushed aside in the mix of all of this and wasn't even acknowledged. I felt a little insecure and upset that I was excluded from the conversation and not even introduced, at the very least. However, I let it slide and tried to put it out of my mind so that we could have a good night out. I figure that what we had was still new and that I shouldn't take it personally.

Once we got into the bar, we grabbed a Canadian and a Long Island iced tea. As we headed for an empty table trying to squeeze through the crowd of people, the women who had spotted you in line came running over and took your hand to lead you to the dance floor. I watched from the table as my boyfriend danced and gyrated against these two women while smiling and laughing. His hands were sliding up and down their legs and hips, even over their asses. I remember making eye contact and being waved to come over and join. I felt so uncomfortable and my chest filled with jealous rage as I shook my head no while tears streamed down my face. You then waved me off and turned back to the women, pulling one of them closer to you. The Long Island iced tea sat on an empty table as I left for the bathroom. I ran into the first stall that was available and sat down on the toilet, trying to take deep breaths in and calm myself. I just couldn't understand why you would do something so insensitive. New or not, we were dating and I was clearly upset. Why didn't you come after me? A new wave of emotions hit me hard, I tried to cover my mouth as I cried because I didn't want anyone hearing me. I continued to breath and be as quiet as I could, but it only took a few minutes for a girl to notice I was crying. There was a knock on the stall door. I wiped my face and opened the door to a girl in a short, leopard print dress. She looked genuinely concerned and asked me if I was okay. A complete stranger in a bar had shown me more compassion than you ever did. I told her I would be fine and thanked her for asking. I don't think she wanted to pry too much, so she just gave me a hug and squeezed me tight. She whispered, or her drunk version of a whisper, into my ear that everything was going to be okay. As she pulled away, I could smell the alcohol on her breath. She stumbled slightly with a giggle as I grabbed her arm to help steady her. She said to me, "You got this girl, now go shake that thang on the dance floor!" She stumbled out of the bathroom with a bottle in her hand. I could hear her excitedly shouting once outside of the bathroom. It made me smile.

I went to the mirror and saw that my mascara had run down my cheeks. I cleaned up my face and took a few more deep breaths. I told myself that regardless of how I felt, this was a new relationship and we just needed to have a talk about it and set boundaries. We needed to establish what we both wanted out of the relationship and maybe I shouldn't just assume things because everyone has different relationship goals. Once we had that talk, I was sure everything would get on track and be fine, this was just a hiccup or a bump in the road.

Something I expected though, was for you to at least be outside the bathroom waiting to see if I was okay, but that's not what happened. When I came out, you were still on the dance floor fondling the other girls while dancing. I thought it would be best if I just left at that point and walked outside. I didn't know how to handle the emotions that were hitting me like a damn truck. It seemed like you were clearly occupied and had little concern for me or my feelings. Funny thing happened though, once I had left was when you decided to come out after me.

You had apologized, reassuring me that it was just harmless dancing with old friends. You told me how much you cared about me and that it meant absolutely nothing.

"I came here with you, not them. If I wanted to go home with them I would, but I care about you and I want to be with you, not them." There was some sincerity in your voice but there was also something else, like you were trying to convince not only me, but yourself. I was new to the dating scene. I didn't know anything about this world and it's boundaries or if I was being too jealous and overreacting. In the end, it seemed logical, he came with me, he left with me, he wants to be with me, and so I thought it was okay. I will try and get it out of my head and move past this. A promise was also made that something like this wouldn't happen again.

Looking back on it now, you showed a disgusting lack of empathy and disrespect that night. They were signs of what was to come and that should have been it. I should have taken that incident as my warning sign and walked away before I got in too deep and got really hurt, but I chose to forgive.

9.

The bathroom door opened. Distracted with my thoughts, I didn't hear the water turn off. The floor creaked with every step as you walked from the bathroom to the bedroom. As soon as the bedroom door shut, I knew I would be left alone the rest of the night. Looking down at my arm, I noticed the blood seeping through the thin, white material of my shirt. I lifted the sleeve, exposing the fresh wound. The burning sensation had faded long ago, a subtle sting left behind. The cut laid neatly above five others. My Obsessive Compulsive Disorder affected the way I cut myself; scars lined up almost perfectly on my left wrist. Dragging my finger across each puffed and white line, I remember the reason behind each scar.

The first was made August 2, 2013. The day I found out I was pregnant with our third child. Bentley, our first child together, wasn't even a year old at that time. I knew you would be angry and I didn't want to tell you, but you would find out soon enough. My morning sickness was horrible, just like it had been for Bentley. You always said you wanted children and made it very clear that you wanted them by a certain age, but even with Bentley, when you found out I was pregnant, you were angry and accused me of cheating and trying to have a baby to keep you around. I never understood why you were always so up and down when it came to children. One minute you wanted them, the next, they were too much and didn't fit into your lifestyle.

When you found out about this baby, you were just as angry as I thought you would be, but one thing I didn't expect was the ultimatum I was given. With no hesitation, you told me we couldn't keep it. You went on about how everyone would be furious with us and how the entire family would end up resenting this baby if we did keep it. It would trap us and completely financially cripple us. I knew you would be mad, but I didn't expect this. You told me that I had no choice and that I had to end the pregnancy. There was no further discussion. It didn't matter that I never supported abortions and it didn't matter how it made me feel. I was wrong to want to keep the baby and I needed to make a grown-up and selfless decision, or so you told me. You told me that I had to be mature and that I had to do this for the family or I wasn't being a good parent or being fair to the other children. "You get this fucking abortion, you need to grow up at some point in your life Victoria and if you have this child, I will leave you in this shit town alone and take the other kids with me. If you can't make the right decision for them, I will make it for you." I remember the vindictive tone in your voice, like I had gone out and got pregnant just to spite you and ruin your life. I felt like I really had no choice. If you had just told me you were leaving, I would have been okay. You knew that though, that's why you had to bring in my other children to get your way.

You wouldn't let up until I had made the appointment. Making that phone call hurt my heart terribly. Every word I spoke, felt like knives being stabbed through my chest over and over. This life I helped create, wouldn't be here much longer, it would be taken away and that thought destroyed me.

Before the ultrasound, I had an appointment with the doctor to discuss what the next steps would be. You were told by the doctor that you were not allowed in the room. This was a surprise to both of us. You weren't pleased and it showed. You gave me a look before I left and I knew that look meant that I needed to watch what I said. The doctor asked me the routine questions. What's your birth date, symptoms, number of pregnancies? He then asked me if I was sure I wanted to terminate this pregnancy. I hesitated, but said yes as I looked down at the ground. The doctor then looked at me and asked me if this was my decision. I looked at the doctor this time. I tried to look confident in my answers and tried to hide any indication that this wasn't what I wanted. I shook my head yes. The doctor then asked me if I was being pushed into the decision at all and he reminded me that it was a safe space to speak freely. I thought for a moment, this was my chance. I could say something. I could save this baby, but I froze. There was too much uncertainty with what would happen. The threat was made. I would lose the children I already had and then what? How mad would you have been if I just told the doctor what was going on and that I was scared? I looked back down to the ground and shook my head no. I knew if I looked into his eyes, he would see the truth. I think he already had a good idea of how I felt, but looking into my eyes as I answered that final question would have been a dead giveaway.

Next was the ultrasound 2 days later. I looked at the screen as the technician did her thing. I remember feeling the cold gel on my belly while she moved around her tool, pushing it here and there. The ultrasound read seven weeks and three days and I could see the waves from the little heart beat, but there was no sound. I never even got to hear the heartbeat. I don't know if that would have made it harder or easier, but regardless, no matter what, I already knew that I loved the little bean growing inside of me. I didn't want to go through with it, I wanted to tell you no so badly. I wanted to scream at you, how dare you put me through this and this innocent child. How could you want to take this child's life away? One you helped create? Unfortunately, I knew the consequences if I did not obey.

August 11th was the day of the procedure. It all felt so fast. I had just found out I was pregnant, had an ultrasound and had seen the little, growing human and now I wouldn't be pregnant anymore. I was sitting in an abortion clinic. Somewhere I never thought I would be.

When I first walked into the room, it was filled with women ready to terminate their pregnancies. I was alone while all the other women had someone at their side. I wasn't allowed to tell a single soul. I had no support. Everything in my body told me to run the other way. Approaching the chair I was given to sit in, my entire body began to shake. The nurse hooked me up to an IV and left me. I looked around the room at all the other women sitting down waiting. They were all different ages, ranging from 16-40, I would say. I noticed they were all sitting and chatting happily with the person they were with, or reading a book. They seemed like they were at peace with the decision they were making because it was their decision. I had the overwhelming urge to scream, but instead I cried. I cried hard. I called you, I said I couldn't go through with it, that I was struggling. I hoped that hearing me so upset, you might change your mind and see how much it was killing me. How much it was truly and deeply hurting me. I wanted you to tell me that it was okay, we would figure it out and to just leave and come home, but you didn't. You told me I had to go through with it, that it was for the best, that we had no other choice, and that I had to do the right thing. I hung up the phone. The nurse noticed I was crying and came over and asked me if I was okay. I couldn't even manage a yes or no, so I just shook my head no. She asked me if I was sure I wanted to go through with my appointment. "It's not too late to change your mind, you can leave at any time." The sincerity in her voice was somehow comforting. I think back to it now and realize it was because she was giving me the choice you wouldn't. I couldn't tell anyone and it was like you didn't care about what I wanted, but she offered me the choice. I looked at her with tears in my eyes. I so badly wanted to tell her yes, I changed my mind and I wanted to leave, but instead I cleared my throat and told her I was going through with the appointment. Nodding her head, she sat with me until I was called in.

When I laid on the cold bed, the protective paper crumpled. I was told to scooch down to the end of the table. Bright lights were shining in my face. My heart was pounding and I felt dizzy. Everything that was being said to me, sounded like it was being said by someone in another room. Sound was faint and my vision was blurry. I couldn't breath. The faint voice told me that I was going to feel a pinch, to try to breathe, and that it would be over in a few moments. I don't even think I responded and then everything hit me at once. That pinch turned into pain. Immense pain. The voices were no longer faint but loud and overwhelming. The procedure only took a few moments like the doctor said, but it wasn't over. The pain never stopped.

In that moment, I believe that I deserved every little bit of pain and more. I took my child's life away. They would never have a birthday, never experience life, never feel the love I had for them. I would never know what kind of human they would have been. All because I was too much of a coward. I had never been so ashamed of myself. I couldn't believe what I had just done. I was a murderer. I tried to stay strong but even days after the procedure, I was struggling. I couldn't eat or sleep and watching you walk around the house fine, like a weight had been lifted off your shoulders, made it worse. You continuously made comments about how relieved you were and that the right decision was made. You saw me hurting and struggling and it felt like you stabbed a knife into my gut and just kept pushing on it more and more. I tried to stay happy in front of Greyson and Bentley. It took everything I had to hold it in until their bed time, when I was alone and could break down.

I didn't deserve to enjoy life. Not to eat or sleep comfortably. I deserved all the pain during and after. I couldn't stop thinking about it every second of every day. My baby would never experience love, kisses, or cuddles from Mommy. They wouldn't ever get the chance to grow up and experience the world, and that is on me. I would be turning 24 in a few days. I would be celebrating 24 years and my baby wouldn't even get one. I wouldn't ever get to hold them in my arms, watch them take their first steps, or say their first words and it's all my fault. I wish I could take it back. I wish so fucking badly that I could go back and do the right thing. I should have told the doctor when I was given the chance. I should have talked to someone, my family or friends. I could have but I didn't, and that will haunt me for the rest of my life. The fact that I could have... but still chose not to.

I was beside myself. I tried writing a letter to say how sorry I was for making the wrong decision. How I loved that baby even though I had to say goodbye. I thought writing it out would somehow be therapeutic. Like maybe it would ease some of the pain within my heart. It didn't. I sat sobbing in the bathroom that night, note in hand. When I reached for the toilet paper on the bathroom counter I noticed the serrated knife I had used earlier to get a tag off Greyson's shirt because I couldn't find the scissors. I had forgotten about the toilet paper I was grabbing and looked at the knife for a moment, noticing the shine the light gave the blade and noticing each and every sharp edge. I don't know what made me pick up that knife, but I reached out for it and pulled it close to my body. I held it tightly in my hands and without much thought, I pulled up my sleeve and placed it against my wrist. It all happened within seconds. It's now a blur. A blur of moments from seeing the knife, grabbing the knife, feeling my skin opening up, and then blood. That was the first time. This was the birth of a new darkness I never knew my heart held. A physical addiction I would pay for.

10.

I rubbed the oldest scar on my arm. The wound had healed on the outside but on the inside, it was still fresh, still burning and bleeding. I covered my arm as I heard little, soft footsteps making their way down the stairs. It was Bentley, rubbing his eyes and half asleep mumbling, "Mommy, where are you?" I called him over as he sleepily stumbled to the couch, all wobbly like someone who had one drink too many. I helped him climb up onto my lap and he rested his head against my chest. Still rubbing his eyes, he slowly faded back into sleep as I played with his thick, brown hair. A reason to keep fighting now lay sleeping in my arms.

As I watched my sweet, little boy sleeping, I felt a shame course through every cell in my body. How could I have let this go on for so long? All I could think about was how I let my children down. How I should have left long ago and done my job as their mother. These kids depended on me and it is my job to help keep them safe and protect them. I feel like I have failed them in the worst way. I knew I needed to protect them and do what was right. I was scared, so unbelievably fucking scared, but I knew what needed to be done. I slowly cradled Bentley in my arms and walked back up to put him in his bed. I gave him a kiss on the forehead and made my rounds to the other two to give them a kiss and pull up their blanket before walking to the door. I looked back and took a moment to appreciate the silence within their peaceful slumber. They were the reason to keep fighting. I had no reason to stay, the abuse had gotten out of control, there was no love, only cheating, betrayal, lies, and abuse. Fear is what held us there, but this was my time to be strong, if not for myself, then for the kids. I knew I needed to suffocate the fear with strength and do what needed to be done a long time ago.

I walked quietly back down the stairs to the living room. Laid down on the couch and began to drift off while thinking about the last few years of my life, why I stayed, and where it went wrong. I was trying to build up courage and erase any doubt in my mind. I thought about the first time I truly felt afraid, and not just normal afraid, but fear for my life and fear of who I was with. You showed me a part of you that I hadn't seen before. This wasn't being afraid of upsetting you or the consequences of not obeying you, this was something much worse. Last year around this time, the name calling had been getting to be too much and you began shoving me and throwing things at me as well. One night, during an argument, I was standing near the wall at the stairs in the living room and I remember feeling chills down my spine as you slowly walked towards me. It was in your body language that I could feel something different in. Your voice became quiet and monotone and the closer you got to me, the quieter your voice became. You backed me into the wall that I stood in front of. Your body pressed against mine. This is the moment I felt it. Even though you had stopped yelling, your voice had become cold and your eyes empty. You grabbed my wrist and placed your other hand around my throat, holding it tight enough that I was unable to slip away. My chest tightened as it became harder to breathe and there was no stopping the tears from falling. Your nose touched mine. I felt your breath on my face as you talked, "stop your pathetic fucking crying. I don't have to be with you and you're fucking lucky I am. No one would put up with your shit. No one would be able to handle your lazy ass. You are nothing but a stupid cunt who grew up in a hick fucking town with no manners. You have one week to smarten up or I am getting my Father to come pick me up with the kids and you won't see them again. I will fight to get custody of them." You then pushed your head against mine pushing the back of my head into the wall. "Do you fucking understand me?"

I remember thinking, in that moment, about how easily my life could be taken from me. How easily and effortlessly you just wrapped your hands around my neck. You wanted me to be gone and you wouldn't have blinked an eye if you were the one taking it. I knew that now. I told you that I understood. I understood a lot in that moment. I had forgotten the hold you had on my wrist and only realized that once the pressure was off. My hand had gone numb from your tight grip. You then let go of my neck and walked towards the stairs. My body went from tense to lose as I watched you disappear into the darkness. I felt the tension build up once again as you spoke from upstairs. "You better sleep in the bed tonight and not on the couch. It's time for you to grow up and stop running away from your problems."

I sat in the soothing, hot tub that night. I sat for a long while, thinking about all your hateful words. This was the day that I started believing you. The day I had really lost myself. The day I stopped believing in me. I thought that I must be the problem. Why else would you hurt me this way? You were always telling me that I just don't like hearing criticism and that I'm in denial of all my problems. That I have avoided working on myself and that all the issues that we had were ultimately my fault. Maybe you were right. In the back of my mind, I thought that even if I was the problem, you said you loved me. How could you treat me this way and say you love me?

11.

I always said love was enough. Always believed that if two people love each other, they could overcome any obstacle in life together and be happy. At this point, I lost belief in that as well. Now I truly understand that you never really loved me. I was convenient at a time where you had nothing. I was there, arms wide open, ready to take on life with you and everything it threw at us. You had seen how vulnerable I was, how naive I was and you took advantage of those qualities. I sacrificed my entire life for you while you stabbed me in the back. I defended you even when you were in the wrong and you threw me under the bus, without hesitation, like I was nothing. You stole who I was and all you did was take from me. With a single touch, you turned my wild and free soul into a black hole within my chest.

I stood up and stepped out of the tub, leaving watery footprints on the bathroom tile. I grabbed the knife I had placed under the bathroom sink, on a hidden ledge in the back, behind the cleaning supplies. I stood naked, water dripping from my hair onto the blade. I had looked in this mirror many times before. Getting ready in the morning, checking my hair or make up, or cleaning the tears and mascara mess. Looking into the mirror this time was different. I had feared what I had become but I couldn't stop it. Instead, I could only embrace it. Embrace the fear and embrace the monster that you had created. I slowly slid the knife across my ribs, watching as the thick and deep red blood dripped down my side. This was me and this is who I was now. How could I allow myself to become such a tortured soul? How could I allow you to do this to me? I continued to watch myself in the mirror. I watched as the tears flooded my eyes, blurring my vision and rolling down my cheeks. I watched as I took the knife and slid it across my ribs once more, right under the first cut. Blood smeared along my skin and the blade. I became angry. I lifted the blade and clenched my teeth, breathing deeply and heavily. Still looking in the mirror at the girl I could barely recognize, I slid the blade against my ribs, this time more aggressively. My breath deepened even more and became louder and harder as I slid the knife again and again and again. Each cut became deeper and more jagged than the last. My hand then began to shake uncontrollably and I lost my grip on the knife. The knife had fallen beside my foot, hitting the floor with a small bang, blood scattered in little drops surrounding it. I held my hands out in front of me, blood covering my right hand and dripping from my fingertips. I grabbed the towel hanging off of the shower curtain and wrapped it around myself. Still shaking, I laid down on the floor sobbing in a pool of my own blood mixed with water. I began thinking about how the fuck one person can have so much control over another. People say words mean nothing, they are just words, right? Sticks and stones, but words mean everything. You decide how to use them and there is power behind every word spoken. You chose your words so carefully and used them to manipulate and hurt. You chose them to deliberately break me. You decided who I was, you decided my fate, and no matter how fucking hard I tried to replace them, those words burned deep within my soul. It was too late and nothing I did could help. The best I could do was try and burn over your words but in the end, yours were still there. It was like visiting your hometown 20 years later and seeing all the changes that had been made since you left. The grocery store was now a Dollarama, the old Beckers you used to walk to with your friend to get slushies was now a Circle K, and the library you snuck into while ditching third period in 10th grade was now a funeral home. However, the signs of what used to be are still there. Behind that dollar store, the old outline of Sharp's IGA laid through the new white and green paint. You could see the old faded sign of what used to be. Even though it had changed signs, the old memories would always be there, just like your words.

12.

Waking up the morning after, I felt like I was waking up from a long night of drinking. I woke up to a bad hangover. I felt sick, I was sore and exhausted, but I was happy to wake up to the kids' laughter and smiling faces. You had slept too, which I was grateful for. I would be beside myself tired or sick but you sleeping in meant the kids and I got a break. This would bug me when Bentley was younger because I felt you should have been helping with the kids as well but now, now I pray you sleep in. Getting out of bed earlier was difficult and I noticed faint red lines on my shirt. I could hear the kids playing downstairs already, so I scurried to the bathroom quickly to assess the damage. The cuts puffed out, and there were at least eight of them slashed across my side. What the hell have you done to yourself, Victoria? I had lost control. There was dry blood all around the area and each cut had already scabbed. I washed it with a little soap and water and added some Polysporin to avoid infection. After cleaning myself up, my next duty was making breakfast.

I snuck into the living room to watch the kids play. Bentley and Jayce had been playing with some Paw Patrol toys while Greyson was building with Lego.

I cleared my throat so that they knew I was there. They all looked at me. "What would you guys like to eat for breakfast?" Jayce was the first to say something, like usual, as he was absolutely obsessed with food. He jumped up and down chanting, "eggs, sausage, eggs, sausage!" The other two seemed to like that idea. So eggs and sausage it was.

I could hear the boys quietly playing as I cooked breakfast. Paw Patrol cars slowly driving on the hardwood floor and Lego pieces moving about and clicking together. For three wild boys, they were fairly quiet and very well behaved. Although, they knew the consequences if they weren't. Not a day went by that Greyson wouldn't get into trouble from you. My heart ached for him. This was also slowly becoming Bentley's daily routine as he was getting older and trying to become more independent and his own little person. In this house, being your own person and thinking freely was frowned upon.

I often drift into my own little world because memories and emotions that I try to repress are triggered. I try to shove them deep down and hide them. Sometimes it's good memories that I try to savour and try to protect from the bad so that I have something good to look back on. Good memories that are tainted with your hate. Lately, it's been hard and those memories have been surfacing a lot. I can no longer ignore them.

I remember that day so well and Bentley's excitement because this was the day I asked about his birthday. This day really hit me and it had sunk in how much they were affected by you and how trained they were by you simply walking into a room.

Once breakfast had been made, the boys all sat at the table. As I placed their plates down, the usual fight of who got to sit where began.

"I sit here Bentley!"

"No, Greyson my seat, that's my seat!"

This always made me laugh because it was a daily argument, at every meal. So, I piped up, as usual. "Boys, you sit here, you there, and Bentley there." I directed them to their seats and they all shuffled around. About two minutes in, before I could get back to washing the dishes, Bentley threw a toy at Greyson and Greyson called Bentley a stupid idiot. I picked up the dish towel and began drying my hands while walking towards the table. Once I reached the table, I lowered myself to their level. "Boys! You guys are brothers and you love each other. Don't call names or throw toys at each other, please. What do I tell you?"

Greyson sighed and rolled his eyes. "One day you won't be here, Mom, and we will have to be there for each other. We are brothers forever, and your brothers are your first best friends."

I smiled at his comment; at least he remembers. "Exactly. You guys are brothers and one day you will have to look out for each other. Even now, you should be doing that. Now both of you say you are sorry and hug it out." They both gave a half-assed sorry and the hug didn't seem loving, but they said sorry, so I called that a win!

Now that they were back to eating, I walked over to the sink to continue my cleaning. I began washing the dishes. As I was finishing the frying pan, I looked over to Bentley eating his sausage. "Hey Benny," he looked over while the sausage was hanging out of his mouth, "you know your birthday is coming up pretty quickly. Any ideas on what you want for your birthday?" The hanging sausage had dropped out of his mouth and onto the table, just missing his plate as he jumped up with excitement.

"I-I- I want, I want!" I couldn't help but giggle at his excited stuttering.

"Calm down buddy, breath." His jumping had turned into constant little bouncing.

"I want superheroes for my birthday!" I began to smile, as if I didn't already know what he wanted. His interest in superheroes began a few months ago. I really wanted to get him a Superman or Batman toy for his birthday, preferably Superman because that seemed to be his favourite. Suddenly, footsteps rushed down the stairs. You walked into the kitchen and Bentley sat back down and continued to eat his food quietly. You looked at me while you zipped up your jacket.

"We already discussed his birthday and what he was to get." I nodded. You then walked towards the front door and were gone.

I didn't care where you were going, just that you were gone. There was always a relief when you left the house. The kids even felt it, you could physically see the change in them; they weren't so on edge. Bentley didn't bring up the superheroes after you had left. He went from happy and talking about what he wanted for his birthday to quiet and submissive. I knew you strongly disliked superheroes, but I was going to get one for Bentley. You always said they were stupid and promoted violence. Just like you thought reading and writing was stupid and a waste of time, they served no purpose. Anything you didn't like or agree with was stupid and not allowed in this household. You were the head of the house, the man of the house, and you were better than everyone else (which you stated fairly often). There were constant reminders of how we all couldn't live without you because we didn't know how to act properly in society. Running around and playing wasn't for kids and that's not how a proper kid should act. They should be controlled and contained.

"Victoria, were you born with a brain? I am pretty sure you were, and I think it be wise of you to actually use that fucking brain of yours for once. Greyson, use your fucking brain and stop acting like an idiot. Bentley, are you stupid?" These were common statements from you. We heard them whenever someone forgot something like to turn off a light, if someone put the toilet paper roll facing the wrong way, or any small little mistake made, really. You believed everything was common sense and no matter how young someone was, they should know these things.

Once breakfast was done and all cleaning was completed, we all made our way to the living room to listen to some music. The boys absolutely loved their music time. We didn't get much of a chance to throw our dance parties anymore unless you were gone, so we took advantage of any chance we got. Greyson loved Marianas trench and Bentley really enjoyed Nickelback. Jayce was my 80's boy and pretty much loved anything with a beat. About three songs into our 80's jams, Jayce wanted to be picked up. He loved being swung about and all the little fancy dance moves we would do. Half way through a Queen song, the door slammed shut. The kids instantly stopped laughing and sat on the couch quietly. Trained, submissive, obedient, smiles gone, and all emotion hidden. The sudden slam of the door made my heart skip a beat and pound hard against my chest. I felt something was wrong and I knew you were mad just by hearing your footsteps. They were heavy and hard, stomping aggressively down the stairs and into the living room.

"I went to the store to get some pop and chips only to look like a fucking idiot because there is nothing left in our account. I know you have some money somewhere, so where is it?" Your statement was more of a demand than a question. You were on edge and had a weird tick within your movements. At the time I didn't realize what it was, but I would find out eventually. I did in fact have money somewhere though, you were right. I had borrowed some from a friend for groceries. I had started hiding small amounts of money in order to be able to feed the kids. I often went without or with very little so that you and the kids were fed. However, you had been spending our money on electronics, games, beer, weed and junk food because according to you, it was the only thing you could stomach lately.

"I have a bit of money for the groceries we need for the kids and their school lunches, but we need quite a few things." I tried to express this in the most calm and genuine manner while walking up the stairs. You followed close behind and I placed Jayce on the floor to go roam about while I grabbed some money. Bentley and Greyson walked up to go play in their room. I handed you a $10 bill from my jacket. I only had $60 and figured that was enough for chips and pop. You grabbed it out of my hand aggressively.

"Why are you hiding money in your fucking pocket and not keeping it in the bank? It's not only your money, it's our money and you pulling that shit is financially abusive toward me. Also, I'd like more than 10 dollars because I wanted to grab a slice of pizza as well."

I was clearly frustrated. We needed groceries and I told you that, but you just didn't seem to care about what the kids needed and it was all about you. "I told you the kids need things for their school lunches for this week and this is all we have until we get paid next. There's things to cook in the freezer or cupboards. I'll even make it for you, but I can't ask anyone else to borrow money." Every word that came out of my mouth was a struggle and I knew there would be an argument. I knew you wouldn't be pleased but the kids needed things and I had to say something. You advanced quickly towards me, which gave me no time to react. With force you pushed me into the wall. My head connected with the wall and a loud thud rang in my ears but I had no time to worry about the pain that pulsed throughout my head. My only concern at that moment was the kids. Looking to my right, I saw the kids in the doorway, completely still, as fear filled their eyes.

"Like I said, this is financial abuse ,Victoria. I shouldn't have to ask for money and you shouldn't be hiding it away."

Jayce cautiously took a step towards us. " Mommy?" he looked confused.

I lowered my voice to a whisper. "Can we please not do this in front of the kids? They are all watching." My attempts to break free from your grip only angered you more. This led to you pushing me back into the wall, hitting my head again, and this time, I had to take a moment to close my eyes and take a deep breath in as the second wave of pain was more intense. I managed to say, "Just take the 20." You tightened your grip on me before releasing. You took the $20 from my pocket and headed for the door.

"Stop acting like a victim, Victoria. Go ahead and cry, throw yourself a pity party. You're the one in the wrong here and someone needs to put you in your place." The front door slammed again. Shame coursed through my body as I forced myself to look over at the kids. I was afraid to see their little faces and think about what must be going on in their minds. I didn't want to cry in front of them, so I held back the tears and instead smiled.

"You guys want to go play sing?" It took a moment, but they loosened up and ran down stairs again. I remember the itch, the itch within my wrist, telling me that I needed to release the pressure, release the pain inside my heart. Even to this day, I have that fucking itch gnawing at me and it fills my body with regret. I wish I never chose this way to cope, but I did. When I get this itch, I just have to open myself up and release the overwhelming pain trapped inside my soul. It's an itch you just can't ever seem to reach and it won't stop until that blade slides across the skin, tearing it open and having that fresh, warm blood seep out. The longer I hold off, the more the urge grows. That day I didn't give in. I was able to curb the urge and distract myself, but it didn't last long.

13.

It was times like this that I would wish I had my sister or Mom to talk to. I wished that I could pick up the phone and just call them. It had been two years since our last conversation. I knew if I contacted them, you would be furious. I was also worried that they wouldn't want to talk to me after everything that had happened and after everything that was said. How was I supposed to message or call them and tell them what was going on? I lied to them for you. I defended you when they tried to warn me. They saw right through you, but I was supposed to defend you. It was my job to choose you.

I missed them. Mom raised my sister Michelle and I on her own. Dad left in the most cliche way possible and we ended up joking about it as we got older. When we were just little, on Thanksgiving, right before dinner, he had left to go get a pack of smokes. He never came back. It was strange that he left like that. At the time, my sister and I didn't see why he would leave his family or why he would leave us, but mom was good at hiding the bad. We knew nothing about their relationship or who our father really was. We never saw or heard from him again, so it was just Mom, Michelle, and I. We were always there for each other. The last time I talked to my Mom, she had gotten into a new relationship with a seemingly nice guy and Michelle had started college.

Even though I missed them, there was still some anger towards them as well. I knew they were right but they didn't help the situation either. They didn't support me, they were pushing me away. I know the situation wasn't the best but why couldn't they just support me? Instead, I was called a disappointment and was being pulled and pushed in every direction. In the end, I should have put up more of a fight when you told me I couldn't speak with them anymore, but I was angry too and knew whatever you said was it. That's what had to be done, but God, did I miss them. I heard Michelle had a baby girl; one that I didn't get to meet. She didn't get to meet Jayce either. I wanted my Mom to be there for the birth of Jayce as she was there for Greyson and Bentley. That day was so stressful and I just wanted my Mom to be there. I had been in labour all day while you worked. You told me that you couldn't leave work and to wait until you got home at 4p.m. When you got home, you started a fight with me and told me that you were leaving. I wanted to call my Mom so badly but I called your Mom instead. Once I made that call, you changed your story and said you were only packing for the hospital. Once off the phone, I sat waiting on the floor near the front door. You walked up to me, got down to one knee and looked me in the eyes. "Are you enjoying the pain Victoria? I hope you are, I hope you're enjoying the pain." That day was horrible. I just wanted my Mom and I wanted my sister.

Back to the present, where the only thing that's changed, the most important thing that's changed, is the realization that hit me like a ton of bricks. I have to leave and it needs to be soon. When I do, everything will be okay, things will get better. Soon, I'm going to reach out to Mom and Michelle because I need them. The kids need them and I want to meet my little niece. I am an aunt, Aunty Victoria. I want that chance.

14.

It had been two weeks since my moment of clarity in the washroom. I still had no idea how I was going to leave or when, for that matter. I had little time to focus on it between all the fighting and planning of Bentley's birthday. The day before was the party and what a stressful day it was. It should have been a happy day celebrating another year with Bentley. It was a small party, just a few friends but I had to plan and decorate and do everything on my own while having you in my ear every two minutes to complain about this or that. You were also pulling me aside often to complain about the guests that were there and to complain about how the children were acting. You could feel the tension in the entire house. People left early because of it and the kids were having a hard time enjoying the party.

To top it all off, I wasn't able to get the superhero present that Bentley had wanted. My heart sank when he realized he wouldn't be getting one. He was so disappointed and that hurt me. I wanted to watch him open that Superman up and see his little dimpled face light up and smile. He may not have gotten that for his birthday, but Christmas was coming up and I was going to make sure he got it for Christmas.

Christmas was my favourite time of year and it was also the kids' favourite holiday. The last few years had been just as stressful as Bentley's birthday, but not this year. I knew I was already leaving. It didn't matter at this point if I rocked the boat. Me breathing and existing rocked the boat more than enough. I could no longer sit by and watch the kids living in misery. So, with Bentley's birthday being over, my mind was set on making Christmas a good one. I loved the magic Christmas held. The warm, fuzzy feeling while sipping hot chocolate and cuddling up to watch Christmas specials with the kids. I always had the tree up early and the decorating done in November. Family and friends would comment on how early I had the tree up, but I didn't care.

I remember when I was pregnant with Bentley that I wanted him to be born into a Christmas wonderland. I decorated extra early so that we could bring him home with the tree up and all the pretty lights. He loved looking at the colours of the tree. I knew he wouldn't remember or really notice and I knew it was kind of silly. My mom laughed at me when I told her. "You are funny Victoria, he's just a baby, he won't even know what's going on." I didn't care. I decorated the hell out of the apartment with Greyson, who was equally as excited as I was.

I still had some time to get Christmas shopping done and I had been saving up some money to get what the kids wanted. What they really wanted. Not what you wanted and liked. I wrote out a list in my notebook. I priced things out and then grabbed the kids to decorate. You were gone working on your so-called business plan and that meant you were gone for most the day. Perfect time to let the kids help me decorate the tree and jam out to some Michael Bublé Christmas music, while we were at it.

During our little Christmas decorating party, my best friend Sharon and her kids stopped by. I had sent her a text earlier in the day mentioning that you would be gone and she wanted to take advantage of that just as much as I did so that we could actually talk and the kids could play.

"How are you doing after the birthday party? You looked so stressed out, I felt bad. The kids were quiet and looked uneasy. I saw that he kept pulling you aside as well, complaining I'm sure." She pointed out.

I sighed a little. "Yeah, I'm okay, it was pretty stressful. He wouldn't stop complaining about every little fucking thing and it was hard to just keep calm and act like nothing was wrong." I would go on to tell Sharon everything, or almost everything. It was hard for me to open up, especially about harming myself, but I knew she understood my situation and would never judge me, especially since she had been going through something very similar. We were there for each other when we could be, we even had a notebook that we would write in and pass off to each other like a journal. We used code names in case someone ever found the book but it gave us something to look forward to, like passing secret notes in class, and it helped us get our feelings out. We would write about everything; happy and sad moments, when we struggled, whatever was on our minds, we would just write and pass it off after a week and keep on going.

I looked at Sharon, I could see everything in her eyes that I could see in my own. "I really am going to be leaving. It's going to happen and I just have to figure out how. I can't live like this anymore. It has to happen and I know I have said it a few times now and never ended up doing anything about it, but this time I really mean it." We both constantly told each other that this was it, this was the last straw, and that we were leaving. However, we always found a reason not to and just hoped for the best and prayed it would get better. We both knew it wasn't going to get better and that one day we needed to make the decision to leave. Sharon and I supported each other and we would support each other through this. We would both make it out with the kids and have a better life. I really believe we met for a reason. We both didn't make friends often, being quiet and reserved and both being in abusive relationships, it was hard to even hold the friendships we already had. We were isolated.

We met at the park, our kids were playing together, and something inside me just told me to ask her for her number so that we could get the kids together some other time, since they got along so well. We got together a week after we met and took the kids to the park. We just instantly clicked. It was as if we had known each other for years. We felt comfortable and trusted each other. We quickly spilled our guts about our abusive relationships and what we were going through. I remember Sharon apologizing because she was crying while telling me about her life. She said that she never does this and that we just met, but we both felt like we were meant to meet. I don't necessarily believe that everything happens for a reason as I'm not a religious person, but I really felt deep inside that we were meant to meet and be friends.

After dinner, Sharon had left with the kids. I took Greyson, Bentley, and Jayce upstairs and started our bedtime routine. We ended the night with a book and kisses goodnight.

You didn't come until late that night and I had already fallen asleep in Jayce's bed. Some nights were easier than others when it came to sleeping but after seeing Sharon, there was always a good night's sleep in store for me. We would figure things out, even if it was one step at a time, and that shed some light and hope onto the very grim situation we were in. That was enough to give me some peace to be able to sleep.

15.

December 1st was snowy and grey. It wasn't even like a new day; it had blended with the day before. I hadn't slept. You argued with me the entire night. There were times I nodded off, barely being able to keep my eyes open and you would just push or shake me awake and continue where you left off. By morning, I was beyond exhausted. When I heard the kids wake, I wanted to cry. Not because they were waking up, but because I had lost the entire night's sleep. Feeling exhausted and frustrated now, I would be awake all day while you got to sleep it off once you were done yelling at me. Because I was frustrated, I ended up using a tone you didn't like and was rewarded with a slap across the face. I didn't even realize what you were doing until I felt a hot sting on my right cheek. I said nothing. I stood silently looking into your eyes. Deep into your soulless eyes. Every time our eyes met, I felt a cold shiver down my spine. No more words were exchanged. You wandered off to bed and I tended to the kids.

I knew this broke a seal into an all new kind of hell. You would lay your hands on me, you would throw things at me, but that was the first time you raised your hand and smacked me. I could see it in your eyes that this wasn't a one time thing. It was only going to get worse after today. New ball game, new rules, and new fears. How much of an understatement that was going to be had yet to be discovered.

The entire day was a struggle to keep my burning eyes open. I had to constantly stay on my feet to prevent myself from nodding off and staying focused on the kids. Later in the day, you woke up on a mission. You came right down to the living room telling me you wanted to speak with me once the kids were in bed. I was already exhausted and the thought of staying up another night triggered a wave of emotion. I cried, but only for a moment. I didn't want the kids seeing me upset. I held the rest of it in and hoped this talk wouldn't be as long as the last.

When we sat down to talk after the kids were in bed, it started off just like the night before and I couldn't take it. I interrupted you this time, risking another smack in the face, but at that point, I didn't care. I just wanted to sleep. I just wanted you to leave me alone, so if the price was a smack in the face, so be it. I couldn't handle another night of lecturing and listening to your damn voice anymore. How much longer do I have to keep my mouth shut and just keep living like this? It didn't matter what I did. I was following every single word you said, but it didn't matter and it never would, so why not start standing up for myself?

"Alright, I am not going to sit here and listen to you lecturing me all night long. I am getting sick and tired of this. If you want to talk about some real issues we have going on, then by all means, please do." My voice was getting louder the more I spoke and my face filled with hot anger. "But, until then, I don't want to hear anything that comes from your mouth. I can't take it anymore. I can't take the way you treat the kids or the way you treat me anymore! You need to just shut up and leave me alone. I haven't slept all damn night and day and now you are at me again! Enough!"

You sat with a smirk and lifted your hand up to your face. I didn't even notice your phone in your hand until then. "Why are you trying to argue with me in front of the kids, Victoria?" I looked down to my left and there stood Bentley. I didn't even realize he had left bed and walked up beside me. You had been recording me and trying to turn things around on me. I shut my mouth and left the room with Bentley. My blood was boiling and yet, I wasn't that surprised you were trying to play these games. I could hear you still speaking into your phone as I walked down the stairs. "Victoria was trying to argue with me in front of our kids, she was name calling and trying to instigate to get me going and arguing with her. She is creating a hostile and abusive environment for the kids to live in."

I kept telling myself to just breathe. Just fucking breath and try not to lose your damn mind. His games and manipulation will get him nowhere. I can't play his games. Just focus on the goal. I sat in the living room rocking Bentley to sleep.

Still on your phone, you kept spewing lies. "She is now downstairs thinking my phone can't pick up her voice as she calls me names in front of our son."

This deep burning rage turned into hopelessness and despair. I picked up my phone and messaged Sharon. I asked if the kids and I could spend tomorrow at her place. I didn't need to explain myself. She said of course and said she would pick us up early in the morning. That was enough peace for me to be able to get some sleep. I curled up with Bentley on the couch and pulled the throw over us. You continued on with whatever you were doing in the room, and your voice slowly faded as I fell into a deep sleep.

The next morning, I woke up before the kids. I left Bentley sleeping on the couch as I gathered up some things from their room and packed a bag. I needed things from my room but you were in there sleeping, so I saved it for last. I slowly woke up the kids and got them dressed and ready to go to Sharon's. They shared their excitement quietly to each other and Jayce asked about breakfast. I told him not to worry that we were going to be eating at Sharon's. Sharon had texted me that she was on her way and the kids were ready at the door. All that was left was to grab my sweater and some pants and we would go. As quiet as I was, you noticed that I had been grabbing things to leave.

As I searched through the closet you spoke up. "Where the fuck do you think you are going?" I had found what I was looking for and as I was grabbing my sweater I responded by telling you that I was just taking the kids out for a few hours. I then felt your hand grip my bicep and spin me around. Startled, I dropped my sweater on the floor. Your long fingers wrapped around my neck with ease as you dug your ragged nails into my skin, forcing me against the hard wall. My bare back and shoulders absorbing the coolness emanating off the wall. You studied my face as I studied yours. For a moment I wondered what it was you were looking for but I already knew what it was, you were looking for fear.

You simpered, gaining satisfaction from the power you had from the fear you instilled. Your eyes were hard. Your skin ashen and rough and the smell of smoke lingered in your breath as you spoke. The tone in your voice was devoid of all emotions. There was no anger or frustration, nothing. It was the lack of emotion that scared me the most. Despite the cold wall connecting with my bare skin, I felt hot, my entire body burning with panic. I placed my hands on your chest, feeling a slow and calm heart beat as I tried pushing you away.

"You are hurting me, please stop." The immense pressure increased as I moved my hands from your chest up to your wrists. A stinging sensation was now present as your nails nestled deeper into my skin. I so badly wanted to scream, cry, or hit you, but even words struggled to leave my mouth and I refused to cry in front of you. I couldn't hold back wincing before the sting became numb and you released some pressure off my neck.

I tried to pull your hands away , enough to allow me to get a few words out. "Please- please stop. You are hurting me." Acknowledging the pain somehow made it harder to control my emotions. You saw the struggle as my eyes became glossy and red. Your smirk turned into a wide smile, showing your crooked and stained teeth.

"You stupid bitch, I will always have control of the most important part of your being, your mind. This won't ever stop." Your grip tightened once again as you took a step towards me, our bodies now touching. Your teeth clenched together and your once emotionless words became complacent. "Run Victoria, get out of here, get away from me. You think that will help you? You will never escape me. I will always fucking be there. When you eat, sleep, fuck, I will always be there deep inside your fucking soul. I will come out to the surface and play on good days, bad days, and when you least expect it. I fucking own you." You let go of my neck and walked downstairs.

For a moment, I stood in total shock. The sound of the kids' laughter from the front door broke my frozen state and I silently picked up my sweater and slid it over my head. I walked to the front door and brought the kids out into the front yard.

As Sharon pulled up, you sent me a text.

Where are you taking the children, Victoria? You didn't even say goodbye. Starting an argument and then running away from it when you can't handle what you started isn't an adult way to deal with things. You need to grow the fuck up and start taking responsibility for your actions. Act like a mother of 3 and stop with this shit. It's getting old. You better be back soon or I will call the authorities for kidnapping.

I clicked ignore. How sick and twisted could you get?

Sharon called the kids over as she got out of the car. "Come on, guys! Play date with Mason and Scarlet!" The kids threw some snow at each other as they ran towards the car. I buckled them in and away we went.

On the way to Sharon's, she mentioned that her spouse, Dave, would be out of town for the next two days. You could hear the relief in her voice as she spoke. Her living situation was no better than my own. She left the kids down at their Grandmother's while she picked us up. Once we arrived at Sharon's, she went downstairs to grab the kids and they all played in the living room while she and I cooked some breakfast. I caught her up to speed with what was going on at home.

"Honestly, Victoria, if things weren't so bad here, I don't care how small of an apartment it is, I would have you guys here in a heartbeat and you could stay as long as you wanted. I hate that you have to go through this."

"I know Sharon, I would do the same with you and the kids. It really is a shitty situation we are both in but remember, we said we were getting out. We have to." I put my coffee down on the table. "I honestly don't know how though. I can't take it much longer. He's mentally torturing me and I feel like I am going crazy with all his fucking mind games he's trying to play. Why can't he just leave or at least stop these cruel games?"

Sharon put her cup of coffee down beside mine and wrapped her arms around me, giving me a tight squeeze. "I'm so sorry, I wish I had the answers and I know you wish you had them too. I think he's a very sick man. He hates himself and is just taking it out on you. He's trying to drag you down to his level and make you feel bad about yourself, but don't you dare believe it, even for a second. You are an amazing Mother and you have been a damn good girlfriend, even when he didn't deserve it. We both deserve better than this. They don't appreciate us. They are abusive to the children and think it's okay because we allowed it for too long."

I shook my head, agreeing with everything she had said. We had allowed it, and for way too long. "I know, I know. I just don't know what to do. I don't know which way to turn or what the right decision is. I know I have to leave and it has to be soon. I am just scared of what he's going to do when I do leave. I don't know how to go about it that will do the least amount of damage."

Sharon flipped the pancakes and grabbed my hand. "I know Vick, me too. I completely understand."

I squeezed her hand back. "You know you are amazing Sharon, and none of this is fair."

Sharon began smiling, her face showed a huge grin from cheek to cheek. You could feel like excitement emanating off of her. "You know what we should do? I think it's time we started saving for a place together. I mean we would save so much money and the kids would absolutely love it. They hate not seeing each other and they all get along so well."

It didn't take much time for me to think about. "I think that's a great idea Sharon, we could be there for each other, be each other's support. Work together and help with the kids, if one of us needs it."

Sharon jumped up in excitement. "Exactly! There would be no more fighting or arguing, we could have a more child-friendly environment for the kids, and it would just be freaking amazing! We both have similar parenting styles, so I don't think that there would be much of a problem in that department."

I took a moment to really let the idea sink in. I didn't want to make any rash decisions because I was in a terrible situation. I wanted to think this out before 100 percent committing to it. I thought hard about it and made a pros and cons list in my mind. We could tough things out for another few months, save as much as possible, and if we are both saving, it could happen quicker. I may even be able to borrow a bit of money from family if I reached out and let them know what was going on. I turned away from Sharon and glanced at the kids. I watched all of them playing in the living room. They seemed so happy, running around with their friends, playing superheroes. Greyson had a towel tied around his neck as a cape. Bentley had put a mask on pretending to be a villain, and Jayce was just running around with everyone else not really knowing what was going on, but enjoying it just the same. At home, they weren't allowed to play like this. At home, seeing them this happy and crazy was very rare.

This was who they were and their personalities were shining through. They were not just robots trying to follow all the rules and walk on eggshells to make sure their master wouldn't be displeased. They were frightened at home. Reluctant to do anything, like playing with blocks or toys, because they were always worrying about the noise they were making.

I turned back to Sharon who was already looking at me. I saw hope and faith in her eyes, her gentle, hazel eyes. I could often see in her eyes what was present in my own. Despair, hurt, trauma, but it wasn't there when I looked at her now. "Yes, I think it's a great idea and we should do it."

Sharon and I shared a smile as she backed away from the table to grab breakfast from the stove top. "It's going to be hard, I know but it's going to be so worth it, Victoria. We are finally going to be free and the kids can just be freaking kids and be happy."

I got up to help place the cutlery on the table with cups. "I agree! We will start looking and saving up. Just don't message about it because he checks my phone and I know you said Dave checks yours, as well. We need to be careful and we need to be smart about it."

"Agreed, we got this girl."

16.

Leaving Sharon's usually brought on a dreadful feeling of going back home to you. Today, when leaving Sharon's, there was relief. I finally had a plan and things no longer seemed completely hopeless. It may not be an immediate solution, but I had a plan. I just needed to hold on until then. I needed to create some space between us. I'll take the kids out more so they no longer have to sit quietly in a house and listen to their parents argue and bicker. I'll get that gym membership I have been putting off for the last year and do something for me. Sharon said that whenever she can, she will pick us up and we can spend the day together. Whatever it takes to get through the next few months, we will do it.

When we arrived home, it was 7:00 p.m. The kids had eaten dinner and bathed at Sharon's, so all I had to worry about was brushing their teeth and reading a book before bed. You weren't home which meant you were meeting up with someone else. That was fine with me. You haven't text me since the morning and clearly the threat you made was an empty one. Just you trying to control me.

Bentley came running down the stairs as I hung our coats and straightened out the boots. "Mommy, I don't want to brush my teef." Ah, this argument was always a fun one.

I smiled while closing the closet door, then turning to Bentley. "Benny, you need to brush all those sugar bugs off your teeth. If you don't, you can get cavities."

This was his cue to start jumping up and down and wiggling his arms about while acting like he had ants in his pants.

"But Mommy, I don't want to! I don't like my teef brushed." He ran back into the room and started jumping on his bed with his two brothers. Time for stern Mommy to come out. I stood in the doorway with my hands placed firmly on my hips.

"Alright everyone, up stairs to the bathroom now. We need to brush teeth and still read a book before bed. No more monkeys jumping on the bed. Monkeys need to brush their teeth now." They all continued to giggle and jump on the bed, completely disregarding me. Now it was time for the count. "Greyson! Bentley! Jayce! All of you better get your butts up to the bathroom right now or there is going to be some trouble!" I put my one hand up and started with my index finger. "1 ...... 2......" All giggles had stopped at the number two and they all ran up to the bathroom. Jayce yelling "three" on the way up. I walked up behind them trying not to laugh. I always found disciplining the kids difficult because half the time, even when they were frustrating as all heck, it was kind of funny. I would be fuming because of their little shenanigans and them not listening to me and still have to turn my face or leave the room so that they couldn't see me smiling. I don't know what it was, maybe their little mischievous smirks and facial expressions, but they always got me laughing and smiling.

After the sugar bugs had been brushed away and their teeth were minty clean, we read a book. The book they all chose was one I would read to Greyson when he was little, Oh my Oh my Oh Dinosaurs. The kids loved it when I read this book. I always made it fun and would tickle them at this one part in the book where they said dinosaurs were cute. They knew when it was coming and would giggle and hide their necks and armpits for the first half of the book. I then started throwing a tickle or two in at random times so that they never knew when it was coming! After reading, I put them all into bed and cleaned up the rest of the house before slipping into a nice, hot bath. There was still no sign of you, no text messages or phone calls. I felt like this was a good time to just relax and pull up some ads on the local buy and sell page, Kijiji, and start looking for a place. Trying to find a house was going to be a challenge. Everything was so expensive, but Sharon and I could make it work. If we split the bills and made a budget for ourselves and just spent our money wisely, I'm pretty confident we would be just fine. We talked about finding a four bedroom house. We would each get our own room and my three boys would share a room and her two kids would share a room. It's a start. The more I thought about the plan, the more hopeful I became. I was excited.

I had browsed a few ads. Four bedroom house for $2000, all inclusive, another four bedroom townhouse $1,400, plus utilities. Four bedroom condo $1,400, all inclusive. The last one caught my attention, it seemed like a damn steal, only $300 more than what I currently pay for a two bedroom! $700 each and it was all inclusive, no extra bills. That was more than doable. It was in a beautiful neighbourhood, somewhere almost in the middle of where Sharon and I were now. I could see the kids making friends with the neighbourhood kids and running around playing tag or hide and seek.

The area we live in now wasn't bad, but this little neighbourhood seemed like the one I grew up in. We lived on a quiet street, where the kids would come out to play with each other. We would play road hockey for hours on end and venture into the little wooded area at the end of the street and hang out in our tree forts while telling scary stories. We were in by street lights on and there was never any trouble or worry. No break ins, no murders, or any horror stories to tell. That's what I wanted for the kids. I wanted them to create strong friendships that last a lifetime, to explore and go on adventures, and to create happy memories.

I decided to send an email out to the last listing. Since there was no guarantee we would get that place, I also sent an email to the other ads I had seen. I thought it was a good idea to keep our options open. I heard the front door close as I turned off the water. I felt a small panic in my chest as I quickly closed off the web browser and deleted my search history. Your footsteps were heavy and loud. I could hear as you unpack your bag, with papers shuffling about, cords and electronics banging into each other as you placed them down on the coffee table. The TV turned on and I knew you were bunkered down for the night. You would spend the next few hours on your laptop while watching documentaries until you fell asleep. This meant no arguing tonight. I finished my bath and climbed into bed. I needed to be up early to take the kids to the park before school to play in the snow for a bit. Maybe I would look up some more ads. I had to keep busy and figure out how to keep my distance from you, not just for my sake, but the kids' as well.

As soon as my head hit the pillow, I felt heavy with sleep. I thought about life and what it was going to be like to be free from you. A house with a big backyard, a cherry blossom tree that I could sit under and read while the children ran around and played. Feeling the cool summer breeze on my skin and through my hair. Gazing at the beautiful white clouds that slowly floated above. Peace, laughter, love, and happiness.

The next morning, with my eyes still closed, I could hear the kids in their room, quietly playing. It was time to get up and pack some lunches. I slowly moved from my side to my back and stretched out my legs and arms. As I was stretching, something was off. I was unusually sore and felt cold under the thick, purple comforter that lay over top of me. Then I noticed an odor lingering in the air, an odor that smelled almost coppery. I opened my eyes and sat up in bed, smelling the air. Could it be something burning? I don't see smoke. I could hear little footsteps running up the stairs. Jayce ran into my room, bounded up and began jumping on the bed. I reached out to grab him but there was red all over my hands and arms. Jayce stood up on the bed and pointed to me. "Blood Mommy, blood." He didn't look scared, he looked more curious than anything. I felt a hot piercing flash jolt through my body as I pulled my arms back and wrapped them around me.

"Jayce, go to your room and I'll be down there in a minute, okay?" Jayce jumped off the bed but instead of walking towards the door he turned back towards me and he grabbed hold of the comforter with both his little hands and pulled the blanket off of me.

"Mommy, blood!" I looked down to see the white sheets soaked in thick, red blood. The copper odor was much stronger now. I couldn't tell where the blood was coming from. I started to panic.

"Jayce, please go play for a minute buddy, Mommy is fine. I have a boo boo. I'm fine."

Jayce began yelling. He still didn't look scared, his chubby little face held no emotion as he yelled again and again. "Blood, Mommy, blood!" I heard footsteps coming from the stairs as Greyson and Bentley walked into the room.

Greyson looked at me. "Grab the syringe and hold her down."

Bentley then walked closer to the bed. "Everything is going to be fine, relax."

What was going on? My sobs became uncontrollable. You walked up to the bed from the corner of the room. Why didn't I see you there before? I heard rushing and yelling. I heard heavy footsteps and voices I didn't recognize, but no one was moving. They were all just staring at me. The voices wouldn't stop and got louder and louder. I placed my bloody hands over my ears and closed my eyes.

17.

I opened my eyes and the room was empty. I was laying in bed on my side. I jumped up and ripped the blanket off of me in a panic. White, clean sheets. I was wearing white pajama pants with green turtles on them. I could see a little rip at the side of my knee where that damn nail on the back of the couch caught me while I was cleaning up the spilled yogurt from Jayce a few weeks ago. Not a drop of blood in sight. It must have been a nightmare. I looked at the clock that sat on the night table beside the bed. 7:00a.m. The kids were quietly playing in their room. I heard tiny little clanks of blocks being put together and sweet, little whispers. I slid out of bed and walked to the dresser. It was time to get dressed and get the kids lunches made and out the door for school. I grabbed the kids some apple cinnamon oatmeal and made sandwiches for their lunches. I also threw in some yogurt, pear slices, cheese and crackers, and a juice box. I added a little pack of Oreo cookies for a treat and zipped them up. Once we were ready, we walked out the door. There was no breeze, just a calm, cool morning.

The kids played for an hour before other kids started showing up. Greyson's friend Jack had come over and asked if they could go to the breakfast club before the bell. I gave him the okay, a hug, and told him to have a good day before he left. Just Bentley and Jayce were left playing in the snow now, throwing snowballs at each other.

8:45a.m. the bell rang. The playground was now filled with screaming children running around in excitement as they all lined up to go in. I kissed Bentley on the head and told him to have a good day. Jayce had started yelling for some eggs, so I knew it was time to head out. This boy and his love for food.

Walking home, I got a text from you.

I expect you to be home right after you drop the kids off at school. We need to talk.

I took a deep breath in and let it go. I picked up Jayce and gave him a big kiss on the cheek. His cheeks were red and warm despite the cool winter day. I gave him another super kiss on the cheek. I always loved kissing his chubby little cheeks. "Alright J baby, we are going to get you some eggs." Jayce shook his head up and down while smiling and wrapping his arms around me. Jayce kept his arms wrapped around me until we arrived at home. Before opening the door, I told myself that this was temporary and that I would listen and not feed into the games. This is temporary. This. Is. Temporary.

18.

It had been days of repeating this is temporary. Through all the arguing and name calling. Through everything I just kept telling myself this was temporary, but the words felt like they had been losing their meaning. I was just saying them to try and make myself feel better about the situation. It meant something a few days ago, but now it felt like empty words. Even when I thought things were going okay after talking things out with you, they never actually were okay. You made me believe they were for a short while, but you would soon remind me, rub in my face that no, it was far from alright. We talked about me starting to go to the gym. I couldn't make that decision alone while living with you because it was still considered our money and it was a financial decision. At the time, you agreed, and I was surprised. One of the conditions of me going to the gym was that I had a friend watch the kids while I went. I was told that I could not rely on you to babysit the kids for me while I did things for myself and had to act like an adult and solve the problem on my own. You expressed that what real people do with kids when they want to go out or work is to find a sitter. So, it was my job to find a sitter for the kids while I went to workout. That was fine because Sharon had already agreed to help me out at least once a week. I could also go while Greyson and Bentley were at school and take Jayce to the play area while I was working out. It was a little extra money, but it wasn't too expensive. I know it seemed silly at the time to think about the gym, it wasn't exactly a priority but I needed something for myself so that I could get out and feel better. I need to let out this frustration and hurt and do something with it. Make myself healthier and better. I couldn't do much of anything else, so this was a step in a good direction, I thought.

I picked a day to go check out a gym. I had not been gone for long and about 10 minutes into a workout, I had received a text message from Sharon to come back home as soon as possible. She continued on and let me know that while I was gone, you were bad mouthing me to the kids and to her. She told me you called your Father and complained about how I was spending all our money on myself and that I was being selfish leaving the kids at home with you when you weren't feeling well. She also mentioned that Jayce had fallen while he was outside and when he went crying to you, but you shrugged him off and ignored him. She picked up Jayce and brought him in to clean him up and was now messaging me. She felt uncomfortable and upset at the way you were treating the kids.

I didn't bother changing out of my workout clothes. I rushed home. Little Jayce was still upset about his fall outside and you were still on the phone with your Father. I picked up Jayce and saw the marks on his hands from the fall. Sharon placed her hand on my back and told me she was sorry he fell and she had to leave soon. It was a mistake to leave them while you were home. They should have gone to Sharon's. I felt horrible about leaving. I thought things would be okay and that it was good for me to do something for myself, but not if it was going to be like this for the kids and for Sharon. I could also tell from the conversation you were having with your Father that you were clearly not okay with me working out at the gym, so that plan would have to be put on the back burner for now. I was okay with that.

After Sharon left, I brought up the issues I had with how things went. This of course started an argument, but I wasn't going to let things slide anymore. It was one thing to bad mouth me to your family and Sharon, but doing it in front of the children and then completely disregarding your own son after he fell and cried for you. No, that wasn't okay. I knew you weren't that interested in the kids and the parenting life. You could barely stand Greyson and only tolerated Bentley. Poor Jayce, you never even wanted him. You said you did, but once you heard I was pregnant, you lost it. With Bentley, you were constantly at war with him, trying to mould him into a mini you and when he fought back with his own personality, not showing interest in the same things you liked, you would resort to name calling and tell him to go away. You shamed him for not being you. A small child, you had no regard for his feelings or him as his own little person.

I tried to stay very calm during the conversation. I was clearly upset about Jayce and how that was handled. But everything I said went in one ear and out the other. You had smoked up while Sharon was with the kids and seemed to be completely out of it now. I ended up walking away because there was no talking to you while you were baked out of your mind. I knew that when we broke up, we would have to co-parent. There would be visits with the kids where I had no say in what you did with them or how you treated them and this frightened me. Even with other adults around, you couldn't care for them. You didn't love them the way I did and you didn't take care of them like I did. You didn't know things like how Jayce liked his sandwich, crusts cut off, in a triangle, and the jam had to be on top and the peanut butter on bottom. You didn't know the books and rhymes Bentley enjoyed or the music they loved. You knew nothing about Greyson because you always pushed him away from the family and tried isolating him. You didn't know how funny and loving he could be and how he wanted your approval so badly. How he tried so hard to earn it, even trying to like the things you liked. You didn't know anything about these kids. It drew panic to think about you being left alone with them for long periods of time because I knew you wouldn't take care of them the way they deserve. I never understood how you couldn't love them. Even if you didn't want them, they are a part of you and you helped to create them. How could you not love them the moment you laid eyes on them? Looking into their deep blue eyes, seeing those cheeky, little smiles, and watching them growing and learning. I just didn't understand.

I joined the kids playing upstairs and left you in your vegetative state down in the living room, in your place on the left side of the couch, watching documentaries while on your laptop. The rest of the day had been surprisingly calm. It wasn't until bedtime that you chose to break that calmness. As I was trying to get the kids ready for bed, you came storming into their room. You had let everything I said to you sink in and now had a rebuttal. When trying to leave the room and take the argument somewhere else, you blocked the doorway. Not being able to leave, I sat on Jayce's bed because he was calling me to hold him. I told you I didn't want to fight with the kids being here and it wasn't the right time to choose an argument. I sighed out of frustration. I then picked Jayce up and placed him in my lap. I barely settled him on my lap when you had walked up to me and smacked me across the face. It didn't matter that I was holding our son. I could only assume it was my sigh that you didn't like or maybe it was because I wasn't making eye contact while you were speaking to me. I refused to look at you. I wanted to hold my face. My instinct was to hold it and comfort the hot sting you left behind, but I didn't want to give you any form of satisfaction. I knew how you enjoyed destroying my soul. I could see it in your face as you called me names and smiled at the tears falling from my eyes. I directed my attention to Jayce. He was holding his chocolate stuffed bunny and handed me his little, blue puppy.

You walked up to Greyson's bed, across from Jayce's and sat down, sitting as far out as you could. Our knees were now almost touching. As you leaned forward, I looked up and our eyes met. It was silent for a moment or two. Then you quietly but sternly spoke. "Why don't you go kill yourself, the kids would be better off without you. You are a terrible Mother, a failure, and fucking disappointment. Do everyone a favour and just kill yourself."

I thought I had seen the darkest parts of you. I thought I had seen frightening behaviour from you, but I don't even know what I would call this. Your tone, your facial expression, and the smirk after the last word was horrifying. The only thing that came to mind was a psychopath. That's the best way I could describe you. I looked into your eyes and thought about the fact that I once loved you. There was a time that I would have done anything for you. I wanted to build a life with you and be with you. I once loved this monster in front of me. I fucking loved unconditionally. Those words sank deep inside. They felt heavy, like I had swallowed a brick. You meant every word you had said to me. That feeling of being trapped grew stronger. Things aren't going to get better. Things were only getting harder and having a plan or not, it was unbearable. I had three amazing reasons to enjoy each and every day, each and every second, but your darkness was taking over and overshadowing those reasons. I was breaking. Any hope had escaped me at that moment.

Maybe you were right. If I just ended my life, the kids wouldn't have to live in this hell anymore. Maybe I really was the problem and I just wasn't seeing it. No matter what I did or how hard I tried, it was never enough and I always messed everything up. I don't learn from my mistakes, I'm incapable of change, I'm stupid, I'm fat and lazy, I'm a cunt, I am a failure, I have no real accomplishments in life, I am a bad Mother, and I am a waste. If I tried to leave with the kids, you promised me a life of misery. You promised that I would regret leaving and that I would wish I was never born. If I thought this was bad, the pain that would be inflicted on me then would be horrendous.

You called your father and immediately began the conversation with, "We need to destroy her, we need to think of ways to take her down." The only way out was to do as you said. Give my children a fighting chance at life. Maybe, if I was gone, your uncontrollable hate for me would dissipate and you would take care of them. You would have room in your heart to love them. Maybe, with me out of the picture completely, knowing I was no longer breathing, no longer living, you would be at peace and finally be happy and be the Father the kids always needed. I don't know why you hated me as much as you did, all I did was love you. I gave you my heart, but your hatred for me was so strong that you would destroy your children just to destroy me.

You had left the room already. Greyson and Bentley laid still in their beds. I placed Jayce down and tucked him in. I then went to check on Bentley. I leaned over him. He looked sad. "I don't want you to die, Mommy."

His words hit me hard. I looked into his deep, big blue eyes. "Mommy isn't going to die, buddy." I squeezed him tight and looked at all the boys, laying in their beds. "Don't worry, guys, I love you so, so much. Everything is going to be fine, okay?" I gave them all a kiss goodnight before leaving the room. I walked upstairs to my room.

I sat on the edge of my bed while the hockey game downstairs echoed throughout the halls. I tried to breath and calm myself down but my hands shook terribly and my head was pounding. I matter. I am not a waste of life. I matter.

Bentley's words rang in my head. "I don't want you to die, Mommy." I tried calming myself, I really did, but then you walked in and saw me struggling to keep it together. I just wanted to be left alone. You walked close enough to knock me while grabbing something off of the shelf near the bed.

"Are you going to continue to throw yourself a pity party up here? You brought this upon yourself, Victoria. This is your fault and you have no one else to blame."

I couldn't take it. The pounding in my head got worse, like a hammer on a nail, just pounding again and again. My face felt hot and my body numb. I stood up and looked at you. I couldn't keep my mouth shut anymore. My voice trembled with every word that had left my mouth. "You need to shut the fuck up and just leave me alone! You are a hor- a horrible fucking person and you just keep pushing and pushing me beyond my limits! You are stealing from me, you're stealing everything that I am, and you are taking my will to live away from me. Do you fucking hear me? I know you're enjoying every little bit of this, I can see it on your fucking face. It's cruel and inhumane. I am the mother of your children!" I couldn't stop. My voice became even louder. I felt nauseous. I felt angry. "I HAVE DONE EVERYTHING FOR YOU AND THESE- THESE CHILDREN. I LO- LOVED YOU AND I- I FUCKING SACRAFICED SO MUCH FOR YOU AND YOU- YOU SPIT IN MY FACE AND CALL ME NAMES. YOU- YOU CHEATED ON ME, YOU HURT ME, AND YOU PUT YOUR HANDS ON ME. YOU TELL ME TO KILL MYSELF! JUST LEAVE ME THE FUCK ALONE, NOW!" I felt like I was hyperventilating. I was trying to breath and hold back the urge to vomit. My cheeks were soaked in tears and my eyes burned. I crossed my arms tightly, trying to control the shake in my hands. When I looked at you, I noticed you hadn't taken your eyes off of me. You picked up your phone and dialed. There was a click and a faint voice.

"Hello, Officer? My girlfriend just told me she was going to kill herself and she told me she would make it look like I had killed her. I fear for her life and I'm extremely distraught and concerned. I don't know what to do." My mouth hung open as a new stream of tears came flooding down my face. The shaking had stopped. My body felt loose and limp. I felt like I was going to faint and the urge to vomit became overwhelming. The entire room was blurry. I didn't even realize you had hung up the phone. There was a loud ringing in my ears as I tried to hold myself up against the wall.

I noticed a blur coming towards me and I managed to get out a few words. "What the fuck is wrong with you? Why are you so sick in the head?" More of a statement than a question. My vision was slowly coming back. You were now standing in front of me. You looked at me with a smirk, with that conniving fucking smirk, but it quickly turned into a frown as you placed your hand on my shoulder.

"It's okay, Victoria. You're going to get the help you need, don't worry. I'll watch the kids while you go to the hospital. You really scared me with what you just told me. I love you and just want you to get help."

My body jerked your hand away. Slowly, I took a few steps back. My hands were now placed on my chest, still trying to catch my breath and just fucking breath. Within minutes there was a knock at the door. You left me in the room to go answer the door.

"Hello, you made a call about your girlfriend, Sir?" I heard a few steps as the officer walked into the house.

"Yes, Officer, she's upstairs in the room." Now my heart was racing. I felt my chest tightening more and more with every step I heard coming from the staircase. When I looked towards the door, I had seen the officer first, and right behind him, you stood.

"Hey, Victoria is it? I've been told you are having a bit of a hard time. Is it okay if we have a chat?" All I could do was nod my head. "Alright, so what's been going on? You told your boyfriend that you wanted to end your life?" The officer looked at me with concern. His voice was kind.

"I never said that I wanted to kill myself. We were arguing and the way things have been lately, it's been hard."

The officer's attention was caught by your waving hand.

"Excuse me, but she's also been cutting herself, Officer, you should probably know that. I am very concerned for her safety."

The officer looked right back at me. "Have you been harming yourself, Victoria?"

I felt like I was going crazy. Like I was actually going mental. "It- it's not like that."

The officer took a small step forward. "I think we should maybe just go to the hospital and have someone look at you. it will give you someone to talk to and assess the situation a little better. I will escort you there and stay with you until you see someone, okay?"

I took this moment to think. The kids were all asleep, and I didn't really have any other option, right? What would happen if I were to say no? How bad would it look on me if I said no and the officer left and when he did leave, what was going to happen with you. Reluctantly, I shook my head yes. I slowly walked downstairs with my arms still crossed. My hands just wouldn't stop shaking. I still felt nauseous and I couldn't stop crying. I grabbed my jacket from the kitchen chair and slid on my boots while the officer waited at the front door. He led the way out into the cold, snowy night. Looking back at the house, I watched as the door slowly closed. When I turned back around, the back door of the police cruiser was open.

"It's a tight fit back there. I know and you're pretty tall, so just be careful with your knees," said the officer as I climbed into the back seat and looked at the bedroom window. I hoped that my babies would be ok while I was gone.

19.

The ride to the hospital was short. It was only a 10 minute drive from the house. We walked into the emergency room together and the officer directed me towards a chair.

"You can go sit down Victoria, I'll speak with the triage nurse."

All eyes were on me as I took a seat in the very busy and crowded emergency room. When the officer came back, he sat beside me. I felt a slight relief being away from you but it also brought anxiety and fear, being away from the kids and sitting next to a police officer in a hospital. I felt embarrassed as I kept noticing people staring at me like I was some sort of criminal. I felt humiliated. I felt angry. I couldn't keep track of all the emotions I was feeling and it gave me a headache. All I could think of was what your end game was here with calling the police, lying, and pushing me over the edge. What exactly were you trying to achieve by doing this? Purposely driving me insane? Drive me to kill myself or force me into submission? Which one was it? And why?

"Victoria Harrison?" The nurse held papers in her hand as she waited for me to join her at the doors.

"The nurse just called you in. I'll be leaving now. I hope you get what you need here. Take care." I thanked him and then walked towards the nurse.

"You are just going to follow me through here to another waiting room, alright?"

I nodded my head and followed the nurse. I had never been in this area of the hospital before. I had heard yelling and screaming many times before, coming from these halls, but never walked down them. It was extremely bright and there were many little rooms with big, heavy doors with locks on the outside. One girl screamed as I walked by yelling for me to help her and let her out as she banged on the glass window. I felt uneasy walking through these halls. Did I really belong here?

We reached a small waiting room where the nurse had asked me to take a seat. Five others occupied the room. Some were sitting with family or friends and one man sat crying, while rocking in his chair alone. I took the only available seat beside him. I sat quietly looking down at my shoes.

"Are you okay, Miss?" I felt the rocking beside me slow down. I looked up at the man, who was now holding his knees tightly to his chest. He looked at me with red, puffy eyes.

I nodded my head. "Yes, I am okay."

The man put his legs down, his feet now firmly on the ground as he leaned towards me. "You look upset, like you were crying. I know things are tough right now but whatever you are going through, you'll be okay." Even though this man didn't know who I was, and he was clearly in his own emotional distress with whatever he was going through, he showed me compassion.

I have always struggled with our arguments and the words that stuck in my head. I had strangers ask me if I was okay and ask me if I needed a hug. Then I have a man who doesn't even know me, show concern over my well being while you purposely inflict pain on me.

I smiled. "Thank you so much. You'll be okay, too." He smiled back at me, placing his hand on my knee and giving it a small squeeze.

"Victoria Harrison?" The man let my knee go once the nurse called my name. I stood up and quietly walked with the nurse to a small, very bright, white room with only three chairs inside. Another lady was already occupying one of the seats. The nurse motioned for me to sit down. I looked around the room once more as I sat. I felt like I was about to be interrogated. Both women had clipboards in their hands and a pen. I already had a good idea about what questions they were going to ask me, but I didn't know how I was going to answer them. I was nervous and this room was so friggin' white and bright.

"Victoria, what brought you here tonight?" I thought about how I was going to answer this question. I was calm until I wasn't. The panic hit hard. Am I here because I am crazy? I have been harming myself and my boyfriend set me up to push me over the edge to send me here? What exactly am I to say? What's going to happen with the information I give them? How mad are you going to be if I tell them the truth? I felt nauseous again. My chest was being squeezed with anxiety and fear. The lights were too fucking bright and these two women were staring at me, waiting for me to answer. I couldn't hold back the tears and the words just came out.

"I- I have been harming myself. I have just been feeling so emotionally distraught and I don't know how to cope with it anymore. I feel that my ex-partner that I'm currently living with is mentally torturing me and tormenting me. He's been getting physical and he's been so mean to the kids. I don't know what to do anymore. I have no control over my life. He's cruel and heartless. I'm afraid that everything I do and say will have negative consequences. I just want it to stop. I just want it to stop." I was afraid but it felt good to finally get it off my chest. I looked at the nurses, waiting for their response.

"That all sounds like it would be very difficult to cope with, Victoria. Have you been feeling suicidal because of this? And have you been harming yourself recently?"

I was handed a Kleenex. Wiping my nose, I answered, "I don't feel suicidal and I don't have plans to kill myself. I just feel so helpless and trapped. I said he was taking my will to live away, I did say that, but that was it. In the past, the thought had crossed my mind briefly. I just thought maybe it would make him stop and I was so mentally torn apart. I don't want to die. I just want this to stop."

The woman that had already been sitting in the room then spoke up. "We completely understand where you are coming from. It's a lot to have to cope with. You're not the only person to have those thoughts or cope by harming yourself. There is help available to you. I know this might be hard but may we please see where you have harmed yourself?"

This was something I didn't think of. Something I wasn't prepared for. I took a deep breath and stood up. I pulled my sleeves up and showed them my left wrist and then pulled up my shirt and showed them my side. The cuts had healed long ago and puffed into white, thin scars. I pulled my shirt down and sat back in my seat. My phone dinged four times in a row. I pulled my phone out of my pocket just enough to see what the dinging was from. I could see the beginning of the messages from you.

Are you almost done? The kids are acting up-

Jayce woke up and he wants you. I need to go to the hospital when you get -

Jayce wants you, so hurry up.

"Is that him, Victoria?"

I nodded to the nurse. I didn't understand why the kids were awake, they were sleeping when I left. Jayce sometimes woke up during the night wanting me so I understood that, but why were Bentley and Greyson awake?

"Well, I am going to tell you that we don't have any immediate concerns with you harming yourself or ending your life. Your charts don't indicate any mental health concerns and I believe your problems are situational. The real concern I have here is you living with your ex under these conditions. Is there possibly somewhere else you could go?"

I shook my head. "My family lives a few hours away from here and I haven't spoken with them in a few years."

The women looked at each other and then back to me. I knew what they were going to suggest and I had considered it, but I just didn't think it was the right decision to take the kids there and have them go through that.

"Have you considered going to a women's shelter? I know it's not ideal, but it would get you in a better environment for the kids."

I nodded. "I have, it's crossed my mind but it's almost Christmas. I don't want the kids to spend Christmas in a shelter and there's fear of how he would react if I left, the consequences. I have been thinking about my options."

The nurse nodded back. "It's good you have been thinking about it. I know it doesn't seem ideal to spend Christmas in a shelter. I get that, but just think about it more. I'm going to give you some information. You can keep it, look at it, and use it how you wish. Whatever you need, at least you will have it, just in case." She pulled some papers from her clipboard and handed them to me. On my way out, the man who had shown me compassion was now gone and a few new people occupied the room.

I called a cab once I was outside the hospital and headed back home. Jayce had been crying for me and was hysterical when I walked through the door. You quickly handed him off. Jayce was breathing heavy, but that slowed down when he wrapped his arms around me, snuggling into my chest.

"Mommy, Mo-mommy." I hugged him tightly as I caressed his hair and moved side to side.

"It's okay my guy, Mama is here. I got you."

You were quick to snap at me. "Maybe he wouldn't be so attached to you if you didn't condition him to only love you." Not even five minutes of being home from the hospital that you sent me to, and already you were starting at me.

I kept my voice low and calm. "I didn't condition him to love me more than you. You don't do anything with him, you don't feed him, wake up with him, or put him to bed. You don't bathe him or play with him. I do everything for him. It's not my fault you failed to create a bond with your own son. I am doing my job and being his Mother, I am doing what I am supposed to do."

You sighed. Clearly not pleased with my response. "Actually it is your fault. You shouldn't have breastfed him as long or as much as you did. You shouldn't have let him use that as a comfort when he was upset. It's your fucking fault and you know it, so thanks for that."

I walked away. I took Jayce back to the kids room where the other two had been sleeping. They looked deep in sleep so I wasn't sure if they were actually awake while I was gone or not, but they were sleeping now. Jayce had settled down and was almost sleeping, so I walked around the room and quietly sang to him as you stomped your way down to the living room.

As much as I didn't want to, I realized it was time to make some phone calls and seriously consider the women's shelter. If things didn't calm down soon, I would have no choice. I just want it to be okay until after Christmas. I really didn't want the kids spending Christmas in a shelter. I knew the kids had been living in this kind of environment for too long. I feel horrible. Sharon and I have a plan but at this rate, I don't know if we can make it that long.

Little snores came from Jayce as I felt his body relax and his head lean on my neck. I laid him back to sleep in his bed and laid down on the carpet in the middle of the room. I looked up at the ceiling fan, watching it slowly rotate, feeling a slight cool breeze. It's going to be okay. I won't lose all hope just yet. I'll keep fighting.

20.

Days came and went since the night at the hospital. It wasn't getting any easier living with you. There was such a negative aura in the house. A hostile environment would be an understatement, but we did make it to Christmas. I recorded most of the morning while watching the kids open gifts. It helped with keeping you at bay. It also helped that you were high on painkillers and marijuana. Even with the medication, the physical abuse became the new norm and more frequent. You seemed to have gotten comfortable doing it, even when the kids were present and as the days went on, you took more and more medication. Soon the kids started asking questions. They wanted to know what the smelly stuff was that you kept taking several times a day, every day. So, you decided to take them all and sit them down in the living room and educate them on what it was you were taking.

I tried to intervene because it wasn't appropriate. They were too young. You snapped back quickly and told me not to undermine your parenting. I was at a loss for words. How could you think that it was a good idea to sit children down and not only tell them, but show them how to grind up marijuana and how to smoke it? In what universe did you think that was a good parenting decision? I couldn't even begin to try and understand the mechanics of your brain and how it worked. I honestly couldn't.

I was furious. I messaged Sharon to ask if we could stay the night at her place again because I just couldn't deal with this. I was so upset. I felt like all you had been doing to the kids was taking away their childhood. Piece by piece, their innocence, their own little personalities, and their fucking happiness was being ripped away from them. They couldn't just be kids. Ever. Jayce was a year old, for God sakes, and he was getting a lesson in marijuana use. What the actual fuck?

It was New Year's Eve and I just wanted out with the kids. I wanted them to enjoy it, stress and drug free. Christmas was just tolerable and only because I chose to record a lot of the morning. However, off camera it was non stop, "hush, stop being so loud, play quiet or I'll take the toy away. Stop this and stop that." You just couldn't enjoy watching the kids running downstairs in excitement and seeing that Santa had come. Waking Mommy and Daddy up to open their presents while playing and giggling. Enjoying their new toys and games. No, of course you couldn't. Instead you commanded and demanded. You complained and tried to control their every move. Every breath. I felt terrible, that's why I recorded. You knew exactly what I was doing. You kept waving for me to turn it off and gave me dirty looks, but I wouldn't. I was taking more of a stand and you didn't like that. It contributed to the hostile attitude and environment, but I couldn't just sit back anymore and let you treat us all the way you had been for the last seven years. I just couldn't.

52 *Why She Chose Life*

wouldn't. I was taking more of a stand and you didn't like that. It contributed to the hostile attitude and environment, but I couldn't just sit back anymore and let you treat us all the way you had been for the last seven years. I just couldn't.

21.

I was hoping the new year would bring something positive and changes would come. I begged for this new year to be our year and for something good to happen to this little family who was silently crying for help. The kids can't live in these conditions and they can't live under constant scrutiny and abuse. It needs to end. They need to be able to be free and just be damn kids for once. Get dirty and run around with nothing but joy and happiness on their faces. It needs to change. It has to change.

The kids and I were ready to go and were waiting for Sharon to come pick us up.

"It's really selfish of you to leave me here alone on New Year's Eve." You sat on the stairs, beer in hand. "Going to a party at your friend's, I am sure you will have fun drinking and flirting with other guys in front of the kids and I'll just sit here alone."

I knew what you were doing. You were going to try and guilt me into staying. "It's not a party. I never said it was. It's Sharon and her kids. There won't be other guys there and we are going so the kids can play and have fun."

You shook your head in disapproval. "Yeah and I wasn't invited. Seems pretty odd and suspicious Victoria, so whatever. Have fun fucking whoever it is that's there. Hope you have fun while I sit alone on New Year's Eve."

Even after everything, there was a part of me that felt bad that you would be alone. "Think what you will, I'm taking the kids for a few hours and we will be back before midnight to do the countdown."

Sharon beeped her horn to let us know she had arrived. So, I hustled the kids out the door as you sat on the stairs, still drinking your beer. On the way to Sharon's, the radio played. "Breaking news, a 36 year old man has been arrested after a disturbing phone call was made to dispatch at 2:00a.m. The unidentified male called in distress about his wife that he claimed to have killed while their three children were in the house. The children have been taken into care by a family member and the wife was taken to hospital with life threatening injuries. She was pronounced dead at the hospital. More details to come." Sharon and I looked at each other. We didn't need to say anything in that moment because we both knew. It's something we feared and could be a possibility for either one of us.

Sharon changed the channel. "Okay, time for some happy music!"

Jingle All the Way began playing on the radio. We spent a few hours playing board games and running around with all the kids. It was loud and crazy, which made it even more fun. If we had stayed home all night, it would have been, "Sit down and shut up, go to your room if you aren't going to show respect and be quiet, don't do this or don't do that," mixed in with an argument with me. When 11:00p.m. rolled around, the stress came back. The heavy feeling in my stomach had returned and I even contemplated just staying, but I knew I was in enough trouble.

When we arrived home, you had been sitting on the steps waiting. The kids and I began taking off our boots and coats as you started to speak.

"Thanks for leaving me on New Year's Eve. That was pretty selfish of you. So, what did you do with your friends? Did you have fun fucking some random guy?"

I quickly motioned for the kids to go up to their room. "Can you not talk like that in front of the kids? What is wrong with you? I left because I needed a break from this shit, this right here. The kids can't live like this. It's not fair to them and it's not right."

You stood up from the second step and walked towards me, your voice becoming lower and monotone. "Well, maybe if you weren't such a cunt and acted like a normal human being, we could get along better."

Blood rushed to my face. I felt the hot rage building. I wish I stayed at Sharon's. "It doesn't matter what I do or what I say. It's always about what I have to change or what I have to do or not do. It's never good enough for you. This isn't what relationships are supposed to be like, I am constantly walking on eggshells with you and the kids are constantly walking on eggshells. You are the one who cheated, remember? You aren't happy and neither am I. Why can't we just leave it at that? Why can't you stop the fighting, think about the kids, and work together? This shit is not accomplishing anything. We don't work but that doesn't mean we can't work together for the kids. If you need support, I'll give it to you. I'll help where I can, but this shit with constantly attacking me and acting this way needs to fucking stop."

You moved closer, your facial expression didn't change and I knew everything I had just said went completely ignored and that things would never change, no matter what. It wasn't ever going to get better.

"You fucking leave, you won't see the kids again and you'll be sorry. I promise you that you will get yours."

This is it, Victoria. It's now or never. I need to figure out how the hell to get us out of this and it needs to be now. You walked into the room and shut the door.

I walked to the kids room to bring them downstairs. I really wish we had stayed at Sharon's. It was pointless to come back home. Regardless, I would have been in trouble, but at least our New Years would have been spent with people we love and who love us. Jayce fell asleep on the couch 10 minutes before midnight. He really tried to pull through with us, but the poor guy fell asleep sitting up with a chip in his little hand. The other two boys rang in the new year with me while you stayed up in the room.

Once the kids were in bed, I went to grab some clothes for bed. You looked up from the computer as the screen lit up your face in the dark room.

"What are you doing in here?"

Our eyes connected. I don't know what you saw in mine, but I saw nothing in yours. Soulless, cold eyes that had once held intimidation, but no more. I was done.

"My children will not live in this kind of environment anymore. I now know that no matter what I do or say, it's completely useless." I cleared my throat. "You have abused my children and myself for long enough. I am done." I walked away, down into the living room with my clothes, you followed me of course as I knew you would. I knew this wasn't going to be easy, but I knew it was something that had to be done. I needed to stop feeding you with my fear and start showing you that I could no longer be pushed around. You yelled at me and threatened me, you told me that you would take the kids away from me, and that I was an unfit Mother. Through everything, I simply ignored you. I had no fight left in me for this. I was done fighting this battle and that angered you more.

22.

You spent 45 minutes on your fit and finally gave up and retreated to the room that night. I knew this wasn't the end of the argument, not for you anyways. I tried to prepare and brace myself for what was to come next. I didn't sleep that night. I had too much running through my mind, too much to think about, like how I was going to pull this off and get out. At this point the shelter seemed to be my only option. It's something I should have done sooner. I put it off far too long. I tried thinking of other solutions, but it just kept coming back to the shelter. Thinking about this triggered my anxiety. Why was this such a hard thing for me to do knowing it's what needs to be done? I knew that I needed to get out, but doubt just kept pulling me and dragging me back. What if you didn't let me leave with the kids and I ended up in the shelter alone, knowing the kids would be stuck in this hell, without me to protect them?

The more that doubt pulled me, kicked me, and consumed me, the more that painful itch throbbed in my wrist. I have to stop giving into them, but the only way to satisfy the itch and make it go away is to take that blade and slide it gracefully and effortlessly across my wrist and open myself up. Tear my skin apart and expose myself. Watch the blood flow out with all the pain drowning inside the red. I was tired of being at war with you, but I was also exhausted with the war inside myself. If I gave in, how long before I would have to answer it's call again? It only gets worse the more I answer. I need to keep letting it ring. I can't do it anymore.

I said I would stop and I meant it. There are better ways to cope. I took some deep breaths in and out. I tried breathing slowly to ride out the urge and it was working, until I heard you on the phone.

Your voice was muffled, you were a floor up and had the door shut, but I could hear every word. "I need to fuck up her life, just like she did to me. She needs to pay and she will." There was a moment of silence and then you continued to speak. "I know a lot of ways we could make life hard for her. I will be calling Children's Aid in the morning and I have a few things planned. Karma is a bitch and she's going to find that out very fucking soon."

I sat in the dark. Jesus-fucking-Christ. I really wish I could call someone for help. I lied for you for so long and pushed people out because of you. I was isolated and although I had Sharon, I couldn't always pile my stress on her because she was going through the exact same thing. Trying to be strong was tiring at best, it was draining and I was pouring from a empty fucking cup.

The urge grew stronger by the second. I felt the shame course through my entire body as I walked to the kitchen. I stood for a moment, contemplating, I suppose, about what I was about to do. I opened the kitchen drawer beside the fridge and pulled out a knife from the back. Your voice continued on in the distance on the phone.

I tried reasoning with myself. Tried reasoning with my damaged heart. Something inside of me was just so fucking broken. I don't know how I will be able to fix it, or if it can be fixed. I tried to stop it earlier but I just need the pain to stop now. I need to satisfy the urge that's gnawing at me. I held the knife in my right hand. I placed it against my left wrist. I don't want to do this anymore. Just please make it stop. I slowly applied pressure as my hand began to shake. My skin hugged the blade. Just a little more pressure and a slight motion downward and the pain will escape. Just one more time. Just…. one… more…. time.

Morning came shortly after and I continued my daily routine with the kids. Wake them up, breakfast, and get dressed. I tried to keep them as quiet as I could. I needed more time to think and not fight. I tried to stay out of your way for the next few days. I listened to every phone call you made to your family and Children's Aid. I listened to all the hateful words you spewed and took it all in.

23.

On the day that everything changed, I followed my daily routine and I needed to get Greyson and Bentley to school. I did everything as quietly as I could because I didn't want the arguing to start yet, but Jayce began crying and screamed when I placed him in his stroller. It wasn't long after that, that you came downstairs, staring me down. You didn't say a word but you didn't have to. I felt what you wanted to say. I felt it throughout my entire body as you glared at me. I left the house with the kids and looked back as you slammed the door shut behind me. You then stood in the kitchen window, middle finger extended. You were keeping your promise by making my life hell and I knew today you were going to really show me just how bad it could get. Knowing that, after I dropped off the boys, I walked a little slower going home. I stopped at the corner store to take a look around just to buy me some more peace before walking into God-knows-what. I knew I would have to face it at some point and Jayce was getting fussy in his stroller, so I needed to get back and let him run around. It was especially cold that day, so staying out wasn't exactly ideal.

When I finally reached the door, I paused for a moment. A panic had set in and next was the fear. I had no idea what to expect or how to prepare for it, but my gut told me it was going to be bad. Opening the front door, I felt those sharp pains of panic and fear, deep in my chest. I pushed the stroller up and into the house. Snow fell from the wheels and onto the tile. You immediately came out of the room and down the stairs. I tried to just continue with my morning routine. Once the stroller was settled against the wall, I tried pulling Jayce out and you walked by me, shoving me into the wall while Jayce was up in the air. I fumbled and slipped on the loose snow settling and melting on the tile. I tensed my arms, trying to prevent Jayce from smacking his head off the wall in the process. I set him down for a moment so I could catch myself. You shut the door behind me and locked it. Fresh panic began stabbing into my chest, fast and hard. My body was slightly shaking and weak from lack of sleep and anxiety. I tried lifting Jayce out again as he fussed. You walked by me, shoving me into the wall again. Jayce was a little higher up this time. I hit the wall, but kept Jayce from hitting it with me. It's like you purposely planned for it to be at that moment so he would get hurt. You walked back up the stairs and once I got Jayce out safely, I pulled out my phone and messaged Sharon. I told her I had to make the call today, that things were going to get bad if I stayed in the house tonight. She told me she would come pick me up with the kids and we would wait at her place until I got through to the shelter. There was no way I could make that phone call and wait in the house with you.

I went to the room to grab a few things. I didn't know how long I would be gone for so I just needed enough things to get us by for a few days until we could come pick up the rest. You stood up off the bed when I entered the room. Jayce was on my hip because once I started to walk upstairs, he insisted on being picked up.

"You have absolutely no business being in this room, so get the fuck out"

I continued towards my things. "I am just grabbing a few things then I will leave."

He stepped in my way, blocking me from my side of the room. "You aren't coming in here, my things are in here and I know how vindictive you are. You aren't touching my shit, so get the fuck out."

I took a deep breath in. "I am not vindictive and not once have I threatened to take or ruin anything of yours. This is my room as well. All I'm grabbing is a few of my things and my bins and I said I will leave."

You picked up the bins on my shelf full of the kids' mementos. They were filled with sentimental and irreplaceable items, but you still threw them across the room at Jayce and I. They had just missed us as I slid over to the slide. "There's your fucking shit, now get out."

"What the hell is wrong with you? You could have hit Jayce! You didn't have to throw it at me. I just wanted a few of my things and I would have left! I am done with your shit, it's not even 10:00a.m and this is how it's going to be? I am calling the police."

You chuckled. "The police? The police can't fucking touch me, Victoria. Go ahead and call them, good luck proving anything. The bins fell off the shelf and I was only closing the door this morning. I never laid a finger on you. In fact, I don't want to be anywhere near you, but you won't fucking leave and stop harassing me."

We both stood there for a moment. I didn't even know how to respond. I just knew I needed out and I needed out today. If I didn't, I was going to end up dead. I placed Jayce down and picked up the items that had fallen out of the bins. I took them, a few of my belongings, and the kids' things down to the living room. Under my desk there was my gym duffle bag. I filled it with what I gathered. Sharon had messaged me that she was held up and couldn't leave yet. I knew I had to make the phone call and I had to make it now. The phone call that I had been dreading for months.

Shortly after, you were walking upstairs and I could hear things moving around and falling to the floor. I had nowhere else to go, I wasn't talking to my family and hadn't for a long time, I wasn't allowed. I didn't have your family for support because of all the lies you had fed them. I was afraid but I knew that if I stayed, I wasn't going to make it. I opened Google and looked up the phone number for the women's shelter. The number appeared and I hesitated. Then I pressed call and put the phone to my ear. My heart pounding with every ring. A lady answered the phone. I tried to speak quietly and tried giving a brief explanation of what was going on.

"I um, I am living with my ex boyfriend and my kids. I-I am, well, there've been some issues with things becoming physical and things are getting out of hand and I think someone's going to get hurt. Things are, they aren't good."

The voice on the other end was reassuring and kind. "I understand ma'am. We are glad that you made this call, we know it can be difficult. Are you okay? Is he with you right now?"

I cleared my throat and tried to lower my voice to a whisper. "He's upstairs. I didn't know what else to do, he's been progressively getting worse with being physical and today he-" I looked up at the stairs and noticed you standing there, arms crossed and a smirk upon your face.

"Are you fucking kidding me right now? You're calling the police on me right now? Like fucking really, Victoria?" He protested.

Concerned, the lady advised me to call the police and call back once it was safe to do so.

You continued on while the lady spoke on the other end. "I am so fucking sick and tired of your bullshit. I am calling the police right now. I am sick of your slander and you aren't going to get away with it."

Choosing to ignore you, I turned my attention back to my phone. "I am sorry, I will do that. Thank you." I hung up the phone as you picked up yours. You paced the room until an officer answered your call.

It took about 15 minutes for the police to arrive. Two officers showed up, one had been here many times in the last while. He knew about the situation and was clearly frustrated that we were still having problems and having to call the police.

"Alright, you guys have been having issues for quite some time now, yes? I don't understand why you are still living together, but this isn't what the police are here for. We aren't here to solve your relationship problems, so here's what we are going to do." You could hear the immense frustration in his voice. "One of you is going to have to leave for the night, I don't care who. I can't choose for you because you are both on the lease, but we are not leaving until one of you decides to leave."

You immediately piped up. "I'm not spending a single night in a shelter and having nowhere else to go, so she can be the one who leaves and figures it out."

The officer looked over in disgust. "Classy" The officer then looked at me.

"Alright, do you have any friends or family that you could stay with for the night or a few days until this gets figured out?"

I paused for a moment. I didn't have anyone. I couldn't stay with Sharon and I couldn't call my family. "No, I haven't talked to my family in a little while and they don't live close by."

The officer placed his fingers on his forehead and rubbed hard, then looked at me with sympathy in his eyes. "I'll contact the women's shelter. I am sorry. I am sure you guys can figure things out in a few days. Just pack for a few days and we will take you there."

I gathered a few more items. The officer that had been here before waited with you downstairs while the new officer waited with me. He looked at me as I packed some clothes, tears in my eyes. This wasn't easy. I didn't want to go to a shelter with the kids, but this was it.

"You know, you're not innocent in this either." I looked up at the officer. He stood with arrogance and authority. His hands rested on his belt.

At first I wasn't going to say anything. I was going to let the comment slide. His words angered me. I am here, packing my things to leave for a women's shelter and he comes into the situation knowing nothing about what's going on and that's what he wants to say to me? "I'm packing my things to go to a shelter with my kids. You have no idea what I have been through, but thank you for that."

He stood slightly less confident. Not much, it was a slight little ease on his shoulders and arms. He said nothing more.

I picked up Jayce as the officers carried some bags to their cruiser. I informed them that we would have to pick up the other two boys at school. I put my coat and shoes on and bent down to do the same with Jayce as you walked by.

The officers were outside placing the bags.

"If I have to push you down to get to the finish line, I will. I'm going to make you wish you were never born. You really fucked up this time."

You walked down stairs as the officer came back to the front door.

"Are you ready, Victoria?" I grabbed Jayce by the hand and shook my head yes as I walked out the door. Bentley and Greyson were surprised to see me and even more surprised to see the police vehicle. They were excited to sit inside and take a ride. We drove away from the school and onto the highway. I watched the house we lived in pass by and become distant. Little did I know, I wouldn't be seeing you for the next few months. I also did not know that I wouldn't be seeing that home for the next few weeks.

24.

We arrived at the shelter and the police officer helped us in. It wasn't exactly what I imagined a shelter would look like. It was very clean and big. There were not a bunch of people like I thought there would be. I guess my vision of a shelter had been slightly swayed by the television shows and movies I watched. I was expecting a big open space with a bunch of people and beds everywhere. It wasn't at all what I expected. There were actually individual little rooms with locks, like a small motel room.

We got a tour of the shelter and the rules. I signed some papers and was given a room. We spent the day mostly organizing things in our own little space and exploring. There was a little park that the kids could play, so we spent some time there as well.

Once the kids were settled and in bed, it hit me hard. I felt like I had failed as a mother. My three children were sleeping in a shelter. I stayed far too long in an abusive relationship and ended up pushing people away because of it. I lost a lot of people. I missed my family and friends. I missed the person I used to be, before you. I walked around the room, watching my boys in their sweet and deep slumber. They had no idea what was going on. They didn't know where we were or why we left home, which I am thankful for. They seemed to think it was like some sort of vacation.

Seeing how they were today, laughing and giggling again, playing like kids should, really showed me that no matter how hard this was, it was the right choice. They are my reason. The reason why I chose life. They are the reason I had to fight back. These boys are everything to me, my entire world. They are my heart and soul and they deserve the best, they deserve to be happy and safe. I needed to protect them from you. This was how I could do that, hard or not, deep inside I knew before that this had to be done. My job, as their Mom, is to do what's right for them. I didn't know what was to come, but at this moment, I didn't need to know. This was the first step of many along the new road we had embarked on. This is where we were supposed to be and we were safe.

Knowing all this, the first night was still difficult. I didn't sleep. I cried and I mourned. I mourned the last seven years of my life that was stolen from me and the years that were taken from the children. The years they would never get back, the childhood they missed out on because of you, and because I couldn't do what needed to be done soon enough. I wasn't only mad at you, but at myself. I was furious with myself. I thought I was doing the right thing. I also thought that you would change, that you meant your words, and it was just taking longer for you to start acting on those words and promises. I knew someone couldn't change over night, so I gave excuse after excuse. You guilted me and made me feel like I was just a crazy, insecure girlfriend. All I wanted was for us to be a family. I tried so hard to earn your respect, approval, and love. I did everything and it was never good enough. I wanted a happy little family. I wanted my boys to have a great Father, the one they deserved. The one who wanted to teach them how to play baseball or teach them to ride a bike. I wanted them to have a Dad who was excited about all of their firsts, just as much as I was. A Father to spend time with and love them unconditionally. To sit them down and teach them how to shave and have the talk when they had their first girlfriend. I wanted Dad and son bonding weekends for them. Going fishing and coming back to tell me all the adventures you guys had, how Greyson caught a real big one, how they helped you gather wood for a fire, and hear about all the bonding you guys had over the weekend. Hear the excitement in your voice and compassion and love for your boys.

They never got that though. You were too busy to ever show interest in them. You were more concerned with moulding them into what you wanted them to be. They were scolded for being creative and different. They were emotionally beat down and they had their childhood and their innocence ripped from their little hands. I remember when Benny wanted to show you something he drew. You waved him off, told him you were busy, and to not bother you while you were working. There was also the time that Greyson made you your favorite animal, a cat, out of clay. You hardly showed interest and later threw it out.

I am thankful for their resilience and how amazing they truly are because even just this one day away from a hostile environment, this one day away from you, they have shown me that they will heal and they will be okay. Their childhood isn't over, they will enjoy it from now until they move on to the next stage in life. Jayce is so small and it's really Greyson and Benny I worry about. Bentley gets so quiet and rigid around you. It's like all emotions are drained from him. I can also see Greyson harbouring the pain. He's seen so much, but I have some hope that we all are going to come out of this better. We all are going to be okay. This is the start.

25.

Morning came quickly. The sun had been rising as the kids shuffled around in their beds, stretching and yawning themselves awake. They woke up with sleepy smiles on their little faces, with their cow-licked, bed-head hair and drool covered shirts.

Breakfast was in 30 minutes out in the dining area, so we all got dressed and ready to eat. They giggled as they slid across the floors in their little slippers, all the way to the first table they had seen. There were only two other women out in the dining area, sipping on their coffee and chatting away. They both looked up momentarily while the kids sat at their seats and then continued with their conversation.

Eggs, toast, sausages, and fruit were laid out in big metal sheets on the large kitchen counter. Plates were stacked to the side with cups for juice, water, or coffee. I grabbed the kids their food first before grabbing a coffee for myself. Since I didn't sleep, I knew I would need the extra little boost.

As the kids were eating, a worker came out from the office beside the kitchen and asked if we could meet after breakfast so that we could discuss a few things. I nodded to the woman and told her of course. I had a few questions myself, so that would be great. She smiled and retreated to the office. I looked back at the kids as they joked about butts and farts and couldn't help but crack a smile at their silly shenanigans. This was the first meal I had seen them truly enjoy in a long time. They were talking and being silly instead of sitting quiet and awkward like at home. During meal times, there was a lot of stress. I had to try and keep them quiet because during meals, they weren't allowed to talk. One of your many rules. They had to focus on eating and they had to eat whatever you said, portion, types of food, even when they were gagging and almost throwing up from being full, you forced them to stay at the table and told them they could sit there for hours until it was done. So, they sat in silence and got in trouble for the slightest noise, coughing, or even chewing too loudly. You critiqued every little thing they ever did and they were always miserable. They got away with a little more while you slept or were gone but now, watching them eating and enjoying their time eating, it felt good. They knew you wouldn't be coming to interrupt. You weren't here, so they could feel safe. It helped put my mind at ease. These moments helped to heal my mangled heart. These moments helped bring back the scattered pieces of my soul.

Once they were finished with their plates, about 15 minutes later, they helped me bring the dirty dishes to the sink and wash them up before heading to the conference room down the hall. A Child and Youth Worker was waiting in the room to take the boys to go play in the playroom, so that they didn't hear all the grown-up talk and I could speak freely. I was slightly nervous entering the room as I didn't know what they were going to ask or what I was even going to say other than a few questions I had. I was a little scared to know the answers to questions like how long we are going to be living in the shelter? I was even more nervous at the thought of talking about the living situation back at home. I had been lying for years about how bad it really was and I had kept the abuse hidden from everyone. I worried about them believing my story and I worried that my kids would be taken away from me for not leaving the situation sooner. Anxiety began to fill my chest once again, and of course, it was accompanied by those sharp stabbing pains. I tried to breathe quietly to myself and keep as calm as I could.

The lady spared no time and started asking questions. She explained that a lot of the questions were necessary to get a better picture on my situation and steps that we needed to take for safety and how they could help.

"What made you choose to leave and come here now?"

I had answered this a little last night but this could give me the chance to give them a little more information. I was in a safe space now and didn't have to worry. "Well… things were becoming progressively more physical at home and I felt mentally drained from all the fighting and everything going on. I knew I had to leave before it got any worse."

The lady took down some notes. "When you say physical, can you give me some more detail?"

This was the part I wasn't looking forward to. Having to explain in detail what was going on. I couldn't even say it out loud to Sharon. I would vaguely text some of the things, but the words didn't really flow easily. "He would throw things, push me… There were times that he would smack me in the face. Things like that."

She continued to write as I spoke. "You said it was also mentally draining, can you elaborate on that a little for me as well?"

As much as the physical abuse affected me, I truly believed it was the mental aspect that was harder than anything. This one was going to be a little tougher to get out. "Um, yeah. It's, it was really hard because…well."

She stopped writing for a moment and gave me a gentle and kind smile. "It's okay, you take your time if you need to. I know this stuff isn't easy to talk about."

I nodded my head. "I felt like I was losing myself and like I was…crazy." She watched me closely while I spoke. "It's hard to describe the exact feeling, but it was like I was going mad. Head spinning, out of control mad. Between lies and the games, it was so hard to see anything positive. I really thought I was trapped and no matter what I did, it was only going to get worse."

She jotted down a few notes and paused. "I can't imagine what that was like. It must have been really hard for you to go day-by-day like that, while trying to take care of the children and yourself."

Yeah, I thought, fuck it was hard. Trying to make it to the end of the day was fucking hard. "It was mentally exhausting. He made me feel like I was insane and trapped me inside this world of his where it was like torture around the clock. Even when he wasn't, I was waiting for it and I knew it was coming, so I felt like it never really ended. I still feel, even being here, that it's not over."

The lady nodded her head and sighed an understanding sigh. "I can't promise you that it's all going to end now that you are out, but I can tell you that it will get better from here. Sometimes it may not seem like it and some days are going to be harder than others, but you got over one of the biggest hurdles. It takes courage and it's not easy. You got out. Just make sure you stay out, you follow the advice given, and you stay strong. We will help you get through this and in the end, it will be all okay."

The feeling of relief kicked in. It was overwhelming at first and tears began to flow as I allowed myself to believe every word she said. We finished up our talk, and discussed a safety plan. Everything was out on the table and plans were in motion. The only thing I was concerned about at this point, was some of my things that had been left at home. I was worried you would destroy them. My computer was also left behind and in the past, you had tried to tamper with it. The computer can be replaced but the kids' baby photos and other things were not as easily replaceable. "Is there any way I could pick things up from the house? I am just worried about things being destroyed and I didn't pack a lot of clothes for the kids and myself." We both stood up and gathered our belongings to leave.

"Of course, we can set up a police escort this weekend and you will be able to pick up whatever you need."

We headed back to the play room where the Child and Youth Worker had taken the kids. It was a very large room with big windows all covered in artwork from all the kids that had stayed at the shelter. I took a moment to appreciate the calm that was my boys. They were usually crazy and chaotic, but Jayce was playing happily in the corner of the room with a doll house and some dolls while Bentley and Greyson were colouring and glueing papers and googly eyes together.

Stepping into the room, it was hard not to admire the very vibrant colours that surrounded you. The drawings and paintings from all the children that had been here, stuck out in the most beautifully sad way. Just seeing how many kids had been in the shelter was heartbreaking, but it was accompanied with happiness that they were saved. That they were given a better chance in life and I hope that each and every one of them got out and lived the life that they deserved. The boys noticed me and smiled, but kept playing. I wanted to take them to the McDonald's down the street and stop at Walmart for a few things so the kids and I had some activities to do in our room.

The Child and Youth worker stood up and clapped her hands. "Okay, Gentlemen! Do we mind cleaning up our areas and then get ready to close on up?"

Surprisingly, the kids listened to the worker without hesitation. They got up and cleaned up their little areas fairly quickly. The worker clapped her hands again. "Wow, you guys are awesome, what a great job!" They all looked quite proud of themselves.

"Hey guys, since you did such a great job, do you want to go to McDonald's, have a Happy Meal, and play in the play place?" I think Greyson was pretty stoked by the news . His mouth dropped as he jumped up and down with excitement. Any mention of McDonald's and he was totally in. Bentley and Jayce were more excited about the play place though. We grabbed all of our things out of the room and went to lock up before we left. The kids were chirping with delight and couldn't wait to get their Happy Meals and run around like crazies in the play area. As I punched in the code to lock the door, my phone dinged. It was a higher pitched ding which told me it was an email. I knew exactly who it was from before even looking at the screen.

"You are fucking pathetic. You are just as narcissistic as your family. You only play victim and you completely destroyed my life. You continue to attempt to put me in jail, so you can keep the kids to yourself. You have no ability to tell the truth. Enjoy your pathetic life. I am glad you cheated on me and I am no longer with you. You did me a huge favour there. Oh, and I will be contacting the police for harassment, remember the slander you impacted my life with is a criminal offence and will be in play if I catch one more attempt of it. Bye. Go live your pathetic excuse of a life. I am happy without you."

At the end he attached a big smiley face. How do I even respond to that? Everything I say he just twists it and manipulates it. At this point does it even matter? I don't even know what he's talking about. This is all part of his plan though, right? He thinks he has a paper trail that makes it true and he can use it against me. I knew it wouldn't make a difference but I emailed back anyways, part of me felt like I still had to defend myself.

"I never destroyed anything and I never cheated. It's really sad that your image is more important than someone's mental well being and your own children. I am also glad that we are done and I am glad that you are happy. You should be happy. We are just two different people and that's fine. I just wish you would own up to what you did instead of lying and playing these games. I also haven't slandered you. If you can't be civil with me then please stop contacting me. Take care."

This wasn't the message I wanted to send. I wanted to say a lot of things to you. I just knew it wasn't going to do me any good. It wouldn't matter if I pointed out how many times you hurt me or how you continued to hurt me. You don't care and, in fact, you take pleasure in seeing me struggle beneath the pressure and weight of your torture.

Once the kids and I left the building, another ding went off. I didn't bother reading this one because I knew it was just some long rant and it was going to ruin my mood. I was sure it was full of belittling and name calling, so I put my phone on silent and chose to ignore it. I had the boys and we were going out to have some fun. As we walked the 10 minutes to McDonald's, there was a slight, cool breeze and light, little snowflakes slowly falling to the ground. The sun peeked through the clouds occasionally, giving a nice warm touch. The streets were nearly empty and quiet, just the footsteps of a mama and her three boys were heard and the little giggles and funny conversations. It was peaceful.

Once we arrived at the McDonald's, we ordered three cheeseburger Happy Meals and a coffee for me. It was surprisingly empty for lunchtime. We sat at a booth inside the play place and the kids ran straight for the play structure. I knew I wasn't technically allowed to, but

I loved playing in the play place with them, so I joined in. I climbed up with Jayce who was overly excited to see me following behind him. He kept stopping to look back and giggle.

"Mommy, Mommy, Come!" Their shrieks of laughter echoed throughout the room. We tried going down the slide all at the same time but ended up getting stuck half way through. Mommy thought it would be a great idea to try out, only to get stuck! Regardless, stuck or not, this was actually really fun. I can't remember the last time I climbed up a slide, but I felt pretty good making it to the top. Bentley waited for me, cheering me on. Bentley was the real climber. He would zoom up the slide in seconds and hang off the bars and climb around like it was nothing. Sometimes it was a little hard to keep up with their infinite amount of energy, but I tried.

We walked back over to the table to grab some of the food before it got cold. Then, my phone started dinging again and again and once more after that. I glanced at my phone and it was showing four new messages from you. Your name in bold, italic letters. Every time I said or read your name, it gave me unease and panic. Just seeing it and reading the words you wrote made me feel as though you were standing right in front of me, looking into my eyes as you held my throat, trapping me against the wall, and leaving me nowhere to run.

I took a deep breath and decided to ignore you again. I knew there would be consequences but right now I didn't care. I wanted to keep playing with my boys and drinking my coffee. I didn't want to think about the shit-show that was our life at that moment. I wanted to enjoy this time, I wanted the kids to enjoy this time, I didn't want them seeing me upset, and wondering why Mommy isn't playing with them or why Mommy looks sad. We were at freaking McDonald's, we were eating crappy food, and playing at the play place. That's all I needed to focus on right now. There was relief in the fact that I could ignore you now. If I didn't want to fight, I didn't have to, I didn't have to worry about going home to you.

So back in my bag the phone went.

"Last one up is a stinky fart!" The kids shrieked as they scurried behind me. The shrieks echoed in the empty play place. This was happiness.

After McDonald's, we headed to Walmart. This was a 30 minute adventure running up and down the aisles looking for some crafts and movies to watch. There was a common room that everyone could use in the shelter, but the TV wasn't always available and there were very few toys to play with. I wanted to be able to relax in our own little place at times and enjoy a movie or some art time with them.

Wreck it Ralph and The Secret Life of Pets were the movies they chose along with some goodies and snacks.

"Mommy, I like this vacation!" Bentley had a huge smile on his dimpled little face. Greyson quickly nodded his head and agreed with Bentley.

Then Jayce started chanting, "'Cation mommy 'cation!"

Although this was difficult on me, the kids really seemed to enjoy it and I was relieved that they had seen this as a vacation. This wasn't going to be a traumatizing time in their life that they would look back on and think, Mommy failed us. That was one of my biggest fears when considering even coming here. I didn't want to fail them.

"Yeah? Mommy likes it too, guys. I'm glad you are having fun." Since leaving the house, the kids hadn't uttered a word about you. They hadn't questioned why we were in the shelter or why Daddy wasn't here. With each day, more and more relief would come. It was just confirmation that I made the right choice for all of us. This had to happen in order to break free and protect the kids.

That night after the kids had gone to bed, I had several notifications on my phone. Four missed calls and I had a ton of emails. Knowing I had already caused enough trouble trying to ignore you, I checked my phone. I opened the calls first. It wasn't you but your father who had been calling me. I think I'll just leave that one.

Next, I checked my email.

It was suggested by the worker that I call the kids every night, so I will be calling them at 7 p.m. starting tomorrow.

Okay, well that email wasn't too bad.

"I expect you to reply to my emails in a respectable time. I know you have your phone and this is about the kids. I know that you like to delegate your time to your new boyfriend, the one you cheated on me with and have your priorities, which clearly talking to my kids isn't one of them, but you need to grow up and act like a Mother and reply to my emails."

There it is. I honestly don't know what you think you'll gain from this. I am in a fucking shelter. What boyfriend? I mean I have to sign in and out of this building and there are cameras everywhere, do you really think that the lies will get you anywhere? They can easily be proven wrong. There I go again, trying to defend myself and you aren't even here.

I didn't bother reading the rest of the emails. I replied with, "OK, 7.pm. works great, thanks." I didn't want to get into an argument or try to defend myself as to why I didn't answer right away. I felt like all I ever did was defend myself. I really didn't have the mental energy and honestly, there was no point.

I did notice a text from Sharon.

"Victoria! I want to come pick you guys up for a night or two, do you think that will be okay? I hate that you are in there. I wish there was more I could do to help. I love you, let me know if it's okay to come get you guys, okay? I know you are busy and have lots going on, so just message when you can! Oxox"

Well, there's a message I was excited to read.

"Hey Sharon , that actually would be amazing. I can go out two nights of the week. I just have to sign out and put the address that we are going to and the phone

number. You can come anytime, the boys are early birds, as you know, and the sooner the better! It hasn't been horrible in here but I mean, it's not home, you know? It is a lot less stressful though, so I can't complain about that. I know you would do more if you could and I appreciate that so much. You have done lots and been there for me. I love you, too. oxoxo. How's your day going by the way?"

My phone dinged after about 2 minutes.

"Well, Dave has been going on and on about how useless I am and continuing to call me names. He also took the bank cards and is refusing to give me money again and I needed to get a few things for the kids to eat. It's frustrating but he won't be here when I come to get you and the boys. He's going out with friends for a few days."

I wish Sharon wasn't still stuck with him. Once I get out of here, I want to help her get away from him.

"I'm sorry, Sharon. We can talk about it when I get there and you can vent all you need to. Things are looking slightly bleak right now. I know it's hard but we both are going to get through it. I can promise you that. Don't forget that you are amazing. Do not listen to his hateful words. I have some money. I'll grab a few things when we come and I'll make a yummy dinner"

I knew that if we kept being there for each other, we could make it.

"I know, we are strong and we can do it! You are amazing too, Victoria. I'm going to go get the kids to bed now but I'll message you tomorrow. Can't wait to see you guys."

I replied back with a, "Can't wait to see you guys too" and placed my phone down on the desk. I did my walk around the room and checked the boys, making sure they were all covered and sleeping comfortably. I felt hopeful. Everything was going to be okay.

26.

The next morning, the kids woke up extra early. 4:40 am. Greyson, Bentley and Jayce had all been jumping on my bed.

"Mommy wake up! Mommy we are hungry! Mommy, Mommy, Ralph!"

If I had a damn penny for every time I heard the word Mommy, I would be friggin' rich by now, able to retire, own my own mansion, and a mansion each for the hungry and hyper butts with Wreck it Ralph playing on repeat. I smiled regardless of how tired I was.

It was too early to go out into the kitchen without them causing a huge commotion and I didn't want them waking everyone up, so I grabbed some of the snacks I had picked up the day before. Bananas, bars, water and some oranges and trail mix. "You guys can have some of this until we are able to go out for breakfast. I can't put on Ralph yet because Mommy doesn't have her computer, but we can colour and play with some toys." I was hoping the morning would go by quickly and that Sharon would text early to come get us. I couldn't wait to just relax and spend time with the kids and Sharon and drink our coffee.

By 7a.m., the kids were rearing to get some breakfast. They were setting out the trays of food and other women and children started making their way to the kitchen. Greyson and Bentley wanted to go play with the other kids in the common room attached to the kitchen, until their food was at the table. I placed Jayce in a high chair with his sippy cup and made my way to the kitchen to make up their plates. There was fruit salad, toast and scrambled eggs, with some pancakes. I grabbed them a little bit of everything and called Greyson and Bentley back over. They came running over. Bentley accidently bumped into Jayce as he was drinking his milk from his sippy and he dropped the cup on the table. That cup then bumped the cup I had for Benny and it dropped to the floor, breaking the cup. The kids all paused for a moment. A few people looked up from their plates to see what had happened.

Jayce broke the silence as he looked down at the cup and pointed, "Mommy, cup fragile."

"Yes buddy, the cup is fragile, that's why it broke." I couldn't help but giggle at this even though I would hear some of the older women going on in the corner of the kitchen, complaining about the kids and how messy they were, and for fuck-sakes this and that. I cleaned up the glass and we continued with breakfast.

The kids were finishing up their plates when I received the text from Sharon that she was going to be coming in 30 minutes. Thank gosh! I had to go sign out for the next two days and get a few things packed. We were all pretty excited and the boys couldn't wait to play with Mason and Scarlet.

Sharon arrived and we loaded the kids in the car. We made a stop at Tim's and a stop at Fresco. I was going to make chicken and some veggie stir fry.

At noon, I received an email.

"I'll be calling at 7 to talk to the kids, so have them ready."

Ah shit, I forgot about the phone call.

"Is everything okay, Victoria?" Sharon had handed me a coffee and sat down beside me on the steps outside the house as the children ran around the yard in the snow.

"Yeah, I just forgot that the kids are going to be calling him every night at seven now, so he will be calling tonight."

"Oh, okay. Well, that's alright. I am here and it will be okay, right?"

I was nervous about the phone call. "I don't know how the kids will react. I mean, Jayce doesn't really know how phone calls work and well, I don't know, but yeah, I am sure it will be fine." I just had a feeling this wasn't going to be as easy as you calling to talk to the kids.

"Yeah, exactly, it will be okay. They are going to have to get used to this now because you guys will have to co-parent, right?"

I nodded my head. "I just wish it was different. I don't even know how co-parenting will work with him. He doesn't actually do anything with the kids. He yells at them and calls them names. With all the threats he made as well, I don't even want to think about them being left alone with him."

"Yeah, I totally get that, that really worries me too. I mean, Dave can be abusive towards me but he's mostly great with the kids. He loves them and he does take care of them, which I am at least thankful for."

I did notice how Dave was with the kids. I hadn't seen him be anything but a loving father to them. Although I wasn't here all the time to see everything, I did see how he treated Sharon. "I don't like how Dave treats you, but I do see him with the kids and I am glad that he is good with them. I really wish the kids' Dad was at least like that with the boys. I mean, whatever, hate me, but if he was at least good with the kids, I would feel more comfortable with leaving them with him, but he just isn't."

Sharon put her arm around me. "It's going to be okay. I am sure Children's Aid and the courts will see what's best for the kids. I know you aren't there yet, but when you are, I'll be there for you."

I placed my hand over Sharon's and squeezed. "Thanks Sharon, I really do appreciate it and I will always be here for you as well." We both smiled at each other and continued to drink our coffee and watch the kids play.

When 7 pm rolled around, I had the kids sitting on the couch in the living room. Jayce was trying to fidget and jump on the couch.

"Jayce, baby, please stop jumping, okay? Daddy is going to be calling any second and it will be hard to talk with you jumping all over." He continued jumping and laughing.

Bentley looked down and then he turned to talk to me. "Mommy, I don't want to talk on the phone with Daddy."

I sighed. I knew the kids didn't want to talk to you but it wasn't my decision to make. "I know, buddy, but don't you miss Daddy? He just wants to talk to you and your brother, ask how your day has been, and things like that. You can tell him about playing with your friends today and having fun in the snow."

Bentley frowned and crossed his arms. "I don't want to."

I looked at my little boy, sulking on the couch as Jayce continued to jump up and down. "Listen, buddy, I know-" and then the phone rang. Jayce had stopped jumping and sat down. "Okay guys, I am going to answer the phone and you guys say hi to let your Dad know you are here." I pressed accept and held the phone on speaker.

"Hello?"

I looked at the boys and pointed to the phone and whispered for them to say hi. Jayce started jumping on the couch again, but managed to say Daddy.

"Jayce, is that you? How are you doing today?" The tone in your voice showed that you weren't asking genuinely, but rather because you had to.

Jayce continued to jump and babble on, not quite sure what he was saying.

"Oh, that sounds cool Jayce. Bentley, are you going to say hi to me?" You could hear the irritation in your voice. Bentley looked at me, he didn't open his mouth and just looked like he wanted to cry. He started chewing on his sleeve as his eyes watered.

"Hello, Bentley? Are you going to answer me? Victoria, can he hear me?" The frustration was quickly turning into anger.

I took a deep breath in and waited another few seconds to give him a chance to say something. I motioned for him to talk, but was unsuccessful. "He can hear you, he's sitting on the couch. Maybe he's just tried."

I could hear you sigh. There was a moment of silence. "Bentley, don't you miss Daddy and want to talk to me?"

Bentley opened his mouth this time. "No"

I knew that I would be in trouble for that. Sharon and I looked at each other. I was about to speak, tell you he didn't mean it that he was just tired after a long day playing with his friends, but I didn't have the chance before you started talking.

"That's not nice Bentley, I miss you. Victoria, take me off speaker now, I need to speak with you."

I wasn't interested in whatever it was you had to say. "I don't think that's a good idea, I am sorry he said that. I will try to have a talk with him before bed."

Your voice was sharp and demanding. The rage you were feeling was no secret. "Take me off speaker right now. I have some words for you and you are going to listen."

My chest began to tighten. "I am sorry, but we shouldn't be talking. If you are done speaking with the kids then we should end the phone call until tomorrow night. I have to get them ready for bed. Do you want to try to talk to them for a few more minutes?"

"Victoria, you better do what I fucking say now or there will be consequences for your actions."

I hung up the phone. I knew you were done speaking with the boys and had no interest in trying anymore. The phone rang. Sharon looked at me with concern.

I answered the phone. "Would you like to say good-night to the boys before they go to bed?"

You answered back quickly, "No Victoria, we will be talking whether you like it or not, I-"

I interrupted you. "We are supposed to have these phone calls for you to speak to the kids, not to argue with me. So, if you are going to try and speak with me and not your children, then I will hang up again. I am going to ask you again, do you want to say good night to them?"

You began yelling, "If you fucking hang up this phone on me again, Victoria-"

Again, I hung up the phone and shut it off. I will have to deal with your consequences later. I was not about to listen to another lecture and you tear me down over the phone. Bentley was afraid of you; he was old enough to pick up on a lot. It brought me back to what he said that night; I don't want you to die, Mommy. He heard what you said, he had seen you pick things up and throw them at me, and slap me in the face. He knew what you were and you hated that fact. They were all very smart boys. Sometimes I thought that they were too smart for their own good but in the long run, I thought that it would help them protect themselves from the emotional and mental damage you inflicted upon everyone that crossed you.

I prayed that these kids were going to be able to bounce back from all of this and be able to come out wiser and stronger. I knew they were just little, too young to understand many things in life, but they understood more than they should at their age. I just hoped that I wasn't too late to let them have their childhood back and be able to enjoy it.

It took about 20 minutes before Bentley was calmed down from the phone call. He was distressed. He closed himself off a bit and stopped playing. I wanted to make sure he was able to go to bed feeling okay. Once he was, I brushed the boys' teeth and got them ready for bed. I tucked them in and gave them a kiss goodnight.

When I shut the light off, they wiggled and snuggled into their blankets.

Sharon walked out of her room and shut the door behind her. "All the kids are in bed. Mommy time!" We headed to the kitchen for some snacks and more coffee before sitting down to watch a movie. "Hey, I think I have some canvases left, do you want to paint while we watch a movie?" I nodded my head and Sharon left to go get the canvases while I cleaned up the living room. We decided to do a water painting of a horse. Sharon was a much better artist than I was and when I looked at hers, it was beautiful. Mine? Well, mine didn't exactly resemble a horse.

"Oh my gosh, what is this? My painting doesn't even look like a horse!" I laughed hard and turned my painting around for her to see.

Sharon then started to laugh. "No, I see a horse when I look at it!"

I looked at the painting again, which started a fresh wave of giggles. "This poor horse!"

Sharon took the canvas "It really isn't bad! But, if you want me to fix it up a teeny-bit, then I can help you out."

My sister loved horses and I remember this collection of horses she had growing up and her favourite blanket had this golden horse with a white mane and tail, and it was beautiful. I tried to paint this horse so that it would resemble that horse.

"Yes, please! I wanted to give it to my sister at some point, just looking a little more majestic and less derp."

Sharon laughed again. "Have you tried messaging your Mom and sister since you have been in the shelter?"

I looked down at my paint covered hands. "No, not yet."

Sharon placed her hand on my knee. "I am sure they would love to hear from you. Maybe they could even offer some support and help, you know?"

I didn't even know how to start off a message or phone call to them. Like hey, sorry I haven't spoken to you in a few years, you were right and now I'm homeless. Then I'd wait for them to say we told you so.

"Maybe it would be a good idea but I just don't know what to say. It's not like they have tried to reach out either, so maybe they just don't want to talk to me."

Sharon was now turned and fully facing me

"Victoria, they are your family, they love you. I'm sure they would be excited to hear from you and that they miss you very much."

They were my family and what do I have to lose, really? If they don't want to talk to me, then they don't and things just stay how they are now. If they do want to talk to me, then I get my family back.

"Alright, I'll send them a message." I turned my phone on to message my Mom and Michelle and noticed more missed calls from you. You tried to call after I turned my phone off. There were some voice messages left that I decided not to listen to. You would be calling tomorrow night at seven again, so until then, I will be focusing on other issues. I was going to message my family and then enjoy the rest of the night with Sharon.

I decided I would just send a Facebook message to my sister first.

"Hey Michelle, just wanted to say hi and see how you were doing. Also thought we could have a little chat and catch up! Wanted to see how the little one was doing too! I'll talk to you later."

I didn't want to completely unload after not speaking for a while. I had to start out short and simple and, to be honest, I still wasn't sure what the heck I was going to even say. This was a good thing though. I sent the message and now I just had to wait for her to get back to me. I had a good feeling about it.

27.

The next day, we woke up to the sound of the kids playing with the motor Jeep. Sharon and I had passed out while watching a movie. Sharon walked to the kitchen to start breakfast. "Crap, I need to grab a few more things from the store. I forgot a couple of ingredients."

I sat up and rubbed my eyes. "Don't worry about it. I can go grab it."

Sharon shut the fridge and walked over to her purse. "Are you sure? I don't mind going. If you do go, I can keep all the kids here and make it easier for you."

As Sharon was pulling out her wallet, I put my hand up. "I got it, don't worry about it! And thanks, it will be faster if I go alone." I knew Dave took her debit card and she probably didn't have much cash on her. She was helping me and I wanted to help where I could. I grabbed my jacket, gave my hair a little brush to make myself look at least half decent, and slipped on my boots. Sharon insisted on me taking her money, but I told her it was fine and reassured her that I had it. I knew that Dave hassled her over money spent even on groceries and we would be eating too, so I really didn't mind.

I walked out into the crisp and cool morning. It was quiet and everything was calm. It was a beautiful morning. The sun was already shining through the clouds and there was a nice, thin layer of fresh snowfall from the night before. You could see some grass blades still sticking out in some areas, but the light layer of snow gave an elegant look to the trees and objects around. I walked down the stairs, leaving footprints on my way down. It was oddly satisfying to step on the untouched snow.

The store was only about a 10 minute walk and I knew that I would enjoy that 10 minutes, just breathing in the fresh cool air and listening to the crunching of each foot step. It was rare to get out of the house completely alone but when I did, even though I missed the kids, I appreciated the little me time I got. I took a little extra time to just look around at the scenery. Even if it was surrounded by houses and cars, I still enjoyed the beauty. I liked looking at the cute, cozy looking homes and massive mansions that made me question what the heck the owners did for a living. I wanted a cute, little home with a nice sized backyard for the kids to play in and have a nice garden with a cherry blossom tree, a quaint little front porch, a little comfy chair and table to sit and read while sipping some tea or coffee early in the morning or late into the night. That or have a nice little farm, grow some fresh veggies, have a chicken or two, and have some other little animals running around. I knew the probability of being able to afford something like that was low, but I loved dreaming. I suddenly felt my shoulder push back and I lost my balance, almost falling to the ground. I looked over and noticed I had walked into someone else. Damn my day dreaming! "I am really sorry, I should have been paying attention."

The man stood up tall, a few inches taller than I was and smiled. "Don't worry about it, I wasn't paying attention myself." As he spoke, I thought about how handsome he was. "Are you out for a morning stroll?"

I cleared my throat nervously before answering. "I am just on my way to the grocery store to grab a few things actually, how about you?"

The man continued to smile as he fixed his grey scarf. "Ah, I'm just walking around the neighbourhood. Visiting my parents and they can drive me nuts sometimes. Escaping for a little to get some air really helps. Don't get me wrong, I love them but man-oh-man, when they get arguing!"

I nodded my head. "Yeah, I understand that! Getting a little quiet time is needed, for sure."

He chuckled and held out his hand. "My name is Jeff. Would you mind if I walked with you for a bit? Burn a little more time before heading back to my parents' place?"

I took his hand in mine, it was warm and welcoming. "My name is Victoria. I wouldn't mind a little company."

We both began walking. I noticed Jeff glancing over at me and when I turned my head to look back, he smiled. "So, do you live around here, Victoria?"

"Oh no, I am just visiting a friend for a few days. I mean, I live in town but not this area. You said you are visiting your parents, do you live in town?"

Jeff placed his hands in his pant pockets which diverted my attention to something else that was very visible in the tight blue jeans he had been wearing. I quickly looked away. Get your mind out of the gutter, Victoria, geeze.

"I actually live just 15 minutes away from here. I visit my parents over the weekend to help them with some things around the house and have dinner with them on Sundays."

I hope Greyson, Bentley, and Jayce visit me when they are older to have a Sunday family dinner. "Awe, that's really nice of you. It's hard nowadays to get families together like that. Everyone is so busy and has their own lives to worry about. Family has always been important to me. I really hope my kids will visit me when I'm old and grey and have family dinners every Sunday"

Jeff threw me another smile. I couldn't help but smile back at that handsome face with a few freckles sprinkled over his nose, perfect white teeth, and hazel, earthy looking eyes. "I am sure they will! Do you have children or are you speaking of future children?"

"I have three crazy boys actually!"

"Oh nice, that must get pretty wild with them all being boys. I bet they keep you pretty busy. So, does that mean there's a hubby in the picture, as well?"

Geeze, how loaded of a question that was. A simple no would do. "Oh, no actually." Jeff stopped walking. I looked up and realized we were at the store. Just then, two police cars went whizzing by down the road with their sirens on. I looked in the window of the first cruiser, he looked familiar, like the officer that had been at the house the day we left for the shelter. The one who made the comment about me not being innocent. The cars took a hard left and were out of sight. Faint echoes of the sirens slowly fading into the distance.

I looked back at Jeff. "I should probably go and grab what I need and hurry back. My friend is probably going crazy with all the kids."

Jeff chuckled and put his hands back in his pant pockets and rocked slightly back and forth on his heels. "Thanks for letting me walk with you. Do you think maybe you would be interested in messaging sometime?"

I paused for a moment before answering. This tall and very handsome man I had run into on the street and walked with me to the grocery store was now asking if I was interested in messaging. Like, this never happens to me. He seems really nice. I am not really in a place for anything romantic, but talking wouldn't hurt, right? "Um, sure. Just add your number in my contacts and I'll shoot you a message sometime." I passed him my phone and watched him enter his information.

"Great! Maybe we can get coffee sometime?" He passed my phone back and shook my hand before leaving. I walked into the store and grabbed what I needed before heading back to Sharon's. On the walk back, I couldn't help but think about Jeff's smile.

"So, are you going to message him?"

I sipped my coffee and smiled. "I don't know, I mean, I don't really think I'm in a good place to be talking to boys. I mean, I'm still in the middle of a bad break up. I don't even have a house to live in right now."

"Yeah, but it's not going to be like that forever. I don't think there's any harm in just talking and getting to know someone. I'll even watch the kids while you go out to coffee. I don't mind!"

Thinking about it, what harm could come from it. I am always up for making new friends, so why not? There's no way in heck I was ready for a relationship. I couldn't even think about that right now, but having someone else to chat with wouldn't be so bad.

"Alright, I'll message him, but not until tomorrow. I don't want to come off as too eager or desperate. I'll just shoot him a casual text tomorrow asking how his day went or something."

"Good! Getting out there and meeting new people is good and maybe it could turn into something else down the road!" She shrugged her shoulders and giggled.

"Yeah, maybe, just friends is fine with me too!" I had to admit though, thinking about messaging Jeff and getting to know him made me feel a little excited but also very nervous.

The rest of the day went by far too quickly. We played outside with the kids and they had a few arguments about who wanted what toy. The day was busy and filled with lots of laughter, messy meals, and snacks. After the kids had had the day's adventures washed off and been put in their clean pajamas, I got them ready for the phone call at seven. I gathered Bentley and Jayce in the room to wait. Bentley was reluctant to come into the room when I had told him what we were doing. It took about five minutes to convince him to come with me. I didn't want to give you any reason to argue or give you a reason to cause trouble, so I asked the boys to please just say hi and a little bit of what they did for the day. I just wanted the phone call to go smoothly and get it over with.

The phone rang at 7:02p.m. I fumbled the phone a little in my right hand before answering.

"Hello?"

Jayce was again the first to say something. "Hello, Hello, phone?"

"Jayce is that you? Hey, are you having a good day?"

Jayce was pointing at the phone with a block he refused to put down for the last hour. "Bock"

"Oh yeah? Are you playing with your brother?"

Jayce bobbed his head up and down. "Ya, 'aying"

"Well, that's cool. Where's Bentley?"

Jayce pointed to Bentley and said, "B here, B here."

"Hey Bentley, how has your day been?" At the sound of your voice, Bentley grabbed the top of his shirt and began chewing. He slunk his shoulders forward and tried hiding his face in his shirt. "Bentley, can you talk to me? I called so that I could talk to you and your brother." Bentley looked at me while his eyes welled with tears. It was the tone of your voice that had really unsettled him. My heart broke for Bentley. "Hello, Bentley, if you aren't going to talk to me then I am just going to go."

Bentley got up to leave the room and Jayce got up to follow him. I motioned for them to wait.

"Hey guys, maybe you should say good night to Daddy before he leaves."

Jayce yelled goodbye instead and left the room. Bentley just continued to look at me, I could see the hurt and pain. A pain that I was also familiar with and a pain that a child shouldn't have to experience. "Bentley waved bye but I don't think I can get him to talk this time, I am sorry." The phone clicked. The call ended. I took a deep breath in and breathed out my nose. The call was over. I wish I could feel relaxed and some relief but the phone call didn't go well. I can't force Bentley to talk. Even with trying to reassure him that you missed him and loved him. I tried to encourage him speaking to you but he didn't want to, he was old enough and he knew. Jayce didn't, but Bentley remembered.

Several minutes later, I received an email.

"I don't appreciate you constantly interrupting the phone call so that I can't speak to my sons. You are talking over everyone which is making it extremely difficult to speak. This is the second phone call that you have not allowed me to speak to my children and if it continues, there will be consequences. Stop trying to impede on my relationship

with my children, it's abusive and you know it. I feel sorry for those children that have to be raised by the likes of you, you narcissistic and abusive bitch"

Even though I knew your words were lies, it still hurt. I couldn't understand why they hurt even though I was fully aware of what you were doing. Why did your words burn so deep within my soul and cause so much damage? This person you described is not me, I know this. I know who I am, so why does it hurt so fucking much?

The kids had been playing in the living room with Sharon. I didn't want to go out and have them see me so upset. I splashed cold water on my face in the bathroom before going back out.

Once the kids were nestled in their beds, Sharon and I put a scary movie on. I thought about Jeff and his smile. My mind even slightly drifted off into another world, thinking about possibilities like kissing that adorable and perfect smile of his. But, that's not why I would be messaging him, I had to keep my mind straight.

I decided to message him though, not wait until tomorrow.

"Hey Jeff, it was nice to meet you today. Hope the rest of your day went well!"

Sharon had noticed me smiling at my phone. "Did you just message Jeff!?"

I could see the excitement on her face. "Yeah, I just told him that I hope the rest of his day went well and it was nice to meet him"

My phone dinged. A message from Jeff.

"Oooohh, he messaged back! What did he say!"

I opened the message and read it off to Sharon.

"Hey, it was very nice to meet you, as well! It was a good thing you weren't paying attention to where you were walking or we would have walked right by each other"

Sharon gave me a very scandalous smile. I messaged him back.

"The one time being distracted came in handy, eh?"

I looked over at Sharon who was still giving me a goofy and weird smile while she made her hands hug and kiss. I laughed at her gestures. "Stop it! He probably doesn't even find me attractive. Maybe he's just a lonely guy who doesn't have many friends and genuinely just wants another adult to have some quality conversation with."

"MmmHmm, sure, Victoria!" Sharon then winked at me and continued to giggle. My phone dinged again and I read the message out loud.

"Very much so! I hope you have a great night, talk to you later."

"See Sharon, that text is the furthest thing from being sexual!"

She waved me off. "Sure sure, he's just taking it slow so he doesn't scare you away. Give it a few days, maybe a week, before he comments on your glowing beauty."

"Ha, glowing beauty, my butt!"

"Oh, don't give me that, Victoria! You are so beautiful and you dang well know it. You were with someone who made you feel ugly, so that's why you don't believe it, but you wait and see. Being out of that, you will start seeing it and you'll get your confidence back."

Some days I thought I looked okay. I kind of liked the way I looked, but most days I struggled. I didn't want to look in the mirror. More often than not, I hated what I saw. I was never too fond of my body and the only thing I really liked about myself was my hair, and even then I could criticize it. Maybe Sharon was right though, she had a point. I couldn't see it now, but one day I might be more confident.

I sent Jeff one last text telling him to have a good night and then watched the rest of the movie with Sharon. I wasn't looking forward to the night being over because I knew we were going back to the shelter. Sharon said she would drop us off after dinner and bath though, so all I had to worry about was getting the kids to bed once we got back. I was happy with the extra little bit of time I could get and we had talked about the coming weeks and being able to spend more time at Sharon's.

When we arrived back at the shelter, the Child and Youth Worker approached me and asked if we could go over some forms and discuss options for the kids' schooling and some next steps. She asked if we could meet in the conference room across from our room after I got the kids in bed around 9:00. The kids were already tired and Jayce had fallen asleep in the car. When I picked him up to carry him in, he had still been asleep. I placed Jayce in bed and brushed Greyson and Bentley's teeth before reading them a little Spiderman book. Once all of them were soundly asleep, I cleaned up the room and decided that since I had another hour before I had the meeting, I would take a quick bath.

As I sat in the hot bath, I checked my phone. There was a message from Michelle.

"Hey Victoria, we are doing great over here, how about you? I was going to message you the other day. I got a weird message from your boyfriend and so did Mom, saying that you guys were doing good and things like that. It seemed a little weird. Thought it was worth bringing up."

What the hell? Why did you message my family? Why would you say we are doing fine? I couldn't even begin to comprehend or understand the mechanics behind anything you did. Nothing made sense.

I replied back,

"Oh really? That's really strange. I actually wanted to talk to you about him. Maybe we can talk tomorrow on the phone?"

I guess there's no point in waiting. I got out of the bath and slipped on some comfy pajamas and a grey oversized sweater before heading over to the conference room. The worker was already waiting with some papers at the table in the middle of the room. I sat down across from her.

"Have you thought about plans for the kids' schooling yet? There's a few options I have here to help you decide what's best for you guys. We could get transportation for them to continue where they are now or there is a school just around the corner from here that we could transfer them to for the time being."

I hadn't really thought about school for them with everything going on. I wasn't even sure how long we were going to be here for, but as it stands right now, it seemed like we would be here for awhile, so it would probably be a good idea to figure it out. I didn't feel comfortable with them staying at their old school because the house was close and I couldn't trust you considering all the threats. The shelter was too far and it would be easy for you to just walk up and take them and I couldn't do anything about it. I didn't want to have to make them change schools but what choice did I have?

"I think I might be more comfortable with them going to the school that's close to here. I am just not sure how long we will be staying here for, so I don't want to switch their schools unless I know we are going to be here a while."

The Worker brought out some papers from her pile and a pen. "Alright, here are some of the forms to fill out for Greyson and Bentley. We can start the process of transferring them to the school close by here and we can process it once we have some more solid answers. Does that sound okay?"

I really didn't want to have them switch. I loved the school that they went to. The teachers were amazing with them and all their friends were there. This isn't a decision that's being set in stone though. Tough decisions are going to have to be made throughout this entire process, this is just one of many. I had to do what was right for them.

Filling out the paperwork, she pulled more out to hand my way. "I know that there's a lot up in the air right now, you are unsure of your living situation, if you will be able to go back or not, but here is a housing form that you can fill out while you are here and we can get you on the waiting list. It's a great start and you can get your foot in the door. You can always decline an offer if the situation changes."

I didn't have much hope of returning home. You were refusing to leave and I wasn't allowed back until you were gone. I was going to have to start over. "That would be great. Thank you so much."

The worker placed her pile of papers to the side and looked at me. "How have you been handling everything, Victoria? Are you feeling okay?"

I hated when people asked me if I was okay. I never fully knew how to answer that question without being so vague and just saying I'm fine. I don't think I have been okay in awhile, so that question just triggered me, I guess. I was in a shelter with my kids and just left an abusive ex. I mean, no, I'm not exactly okay, but I am better than I was a week ago. It wasn't ideal being in a shelter but it wasn't ideal living with the abuse either.

"It's been hard, but I have been managing."

She nodded her head. I knew she understood exactly how I felt. "If you ever need to talk to anyone, we have a councillor here every Tuesday and Thursday. You can make appointments at the front desk with whoever is on shift. We are here to help in any way that we can to get you and the children through all of this. We want you guys to feel safe and supported. We also want to see you guys succeed and be able to move on from what has happened. You have support here! You don't need to do this alone and you don't have to feel like you have to keep everything to yourself. Anything you need, just let us know."

I smiled back at her. I knew they were here to help. We felt very welcome and the staff had been very nice and sincere. It's really helped the process, that's for sure. "Thank you, I really appreciate that, I will take you up on the offer and book a session with the counsellor." I knew I needed to talk to someone and get everything off my chest. Thinking about talking about it with someone gave me anxiety. I was only ever able to speak with Sharon about what had been going on and even that was sometimes hard to do. I was conditioned to keep my emotions and feelings to myself and I was afraid to share them. Not having my feelings validated or getting in trouble for having emotions can put a toll on you. Anytime I had been upset or angry about something, it would always start an argument. I really tried to be level headed with my emotions, not let them take over and just bring up what was bothering me, but it didn't matter how nice I was about it, I would get in trouble.

So, I just learned to keep it all to myself. I wouldn't get in trouble or start a fight if I was just the obedient girlfriend. Things would be okay if I played that role, but even so, things were never better. I could be walking around on all fours, kissing your feet, listening and fulfilling every command you barked at me, and it wouldn't make a difference.

All of this gnaws at me. The thoughts that invade my mind daily, and the more I tried to push it down, the worse it got. It's part of the reason I chose to cut myself. It helped relieve some of the pain and helped me keep my feelings and emotions at bay. Was it a great decision? No, it really wasn't. I left my body scarred for the rest of my life. I left reminders on my body of all the pain and suffering but I didn't know how else to cope and the last time I had tried counselling, it led to nothing but accusations. I had to stop, there was no point in going and not being allowed to talk about my feelings. You had coached me about what to talk about before each appointment and even then, you would question everything I had said to the counsellor and that stressed me out even more. Regardless, this was a step forward and a step towards bettering myself and the situation. It was going to be a struggle to talk about certain things. I knew that, but I needed this. I was not weak for seeking help. I was not weak for feeling and having emotions. This was strength. I am confronting my demons, so they can no longer taunt me. I would do anything to get rid of them, to not have them stabbing my insides with their poisonous daggers, poison that entered my bloodstream and coursed throughout my entire body, taking over my being and creating urges, like the one that itches my wrist dreadfully. The urges that made me pick up a serrated knife to cut open my wrists, trying to release the poison within. Because once all is said and done, that poison is trapped inside once the wounds heal and I am left with ugly fucking scars.

Cutting didn't help. This was mental and that's where I needed to start in order to heal. Bleeding wasn't going to fix me. It wasn't going to fix the situation. You planted these demons inside me because they weren't there before we met. I didn't even fully realize they were there until I was standing naked and wet in front of the mirror, knife in hand, blood seeping from my side, down my body, and onto the floor. I was looking at myself in the mirror, but it really wasn't me. I acknowledged the demons in that moment and that's when they really took hold of me. I could see it in my eyes and felt it in my heart, that I was no longer me. I thought that I was gone but I realize now that I was lost inside myself. I hid my true self deep within my soul, trying to protect the girl I was. I was in there, afraid and alone just trying to survive and trying to protect what little I had left. Protecting the love and hope that I held so dear and close to my heart. The love and hope that fueled my entire being. I came back though. I may have been bloodied and bruised, but I was in one piece. I was me again and that hope and love was still there.

I walked back to my room where the kids were still soundly asleep. My phone vibrated in my house coat. I fished it out of my pocket, it was a message from Jeff.

"Hey Victoria, hope you had a good day today!"

Very simple. Nothing outrageous or charming yet, but still able to make me smile.

"Hey Jeff, I had a pretty good day with the kids and Sharon. I hope yours was good too!"

Geeze I am lame, nice reply, Victoria. Jeff replied back after a moment:

"My day has been great! I can't stop thinking about our walk to the store though. I was thinking maybe if you weren't too busy this week, maybe on Wednesday, we could meet up for a coffee?"

He can't stop thinking about our walk to the store! Oh man, maybe Sharon was right. I don't know how to feel about that one. Maybe I am reading too much into it?

"Oh yeah? I think coffee would be a great idea, let me make sure Wednesday works"

This wouldn't be considered a date, right? It's just coffee with an acquaintance, not even a friend yet.

"Awesome! It's a date! Well possibly, if you are able to make it that is."

Shit. well that's just a figure of speech, that doesn't mean it's an actual date.

"I'll let you know tomorrow. Have a good night"

I messaged Sharon after to ask if she was able to watch the boys for the coffee date. I knew she was going to be thrilled and make a big deal about it. Damn it, I said coffee date. It's not a date, it's just coffee. She messaged me back with an of course, which I knew she would.

I plugged my phone in to charge and decided to go to bed. The kids always woke up early and there was so much work that needed to be done. I checked all the boys, made my rounds, kissed their sleepy heads, and then laid in bed. I looked up at the ceiling and thought about Mom and Michelle. I hadn't yet messaged Mom but I talked to Michelle about a phone call. I wonder how it would go. How she would feel. We added each other on Facebook and I looked through some of the pictures of my niece. She was so cute and around Jayce's age. You could tell they were cousins. I wonder if she knows about Aunt Victoria and her three cousins. So many questions, but in time we will see. For now, I need to get some rest. I need sleep. I pulled the covers up to my chin and turned onto my side. I reached over to the table beside my bed and clicked the light off. The little room was devoured by the darkness. The moon shined in through the tall, leafless trees covered in snow and ice outside and the little window above the bed. It drew shadows on the wall across from me, tall scary figures that might scare a child alone in the dark. I wasn't afraid of the monsters under the bed anymore. I closed my eyes.

28.

Greyson sat on the edge of his bed. Bentley was crying. I saw Jayce running around. Greyson had his arms wrapped around Bentley, something I didn't see very often. They were usually fighting and hitting each other. Bentley tried speaking through muffled tears as his face lay into Greyson's chest.

"I don't want Mommy to die Grey- Greyson."

Greyson rubbed his hair. Jayce was running around saying Mommy, Mommy, Mommy over and over again.

I walked into the room to comfort Benny. "Guys, I won't die, please don't be upset." They wouldn't look at me. I went to touch Greyson's shoulder.

Greyson looked at me. Bentley raised his head, his eyes puffy and red. "Why did you die, Mommy?"

I felt so confused. "Baby, I didn't die, I am right here."

Jayce was running around behind me. "Mommy die, Mommy die, Mommy die."

I grabbed his arm and picked him up. "Jayce, don't say that, baby. I am not going to die. I am right here buddy."

Jayce then started crying. "Mom, come home."

I gave him a super kiss on his chubby cheeks as I started crying. "Buddy, Mommy is right here. I am home."

Bentley started crying hysterically. "I want my Mom. Why can't she be here?!"

Greyson hugged Bentley again. "It's okay, Benny, I love you. I am here for you. Remember when Mommy said one day she won't be here, we have to be there for each other? I am here for you and Jayce."

I looked at them all again, through blurred tearful eyes. They were all wearing black suits. We weren't at home. Where were we? "Guys, please stop being sad, Mommy is right here, please. Mommy gave you a super kiss Jayce baby, it's okay."

I heard the voices again, those loud overwhelming voices. "Grab the syringe."

Scurrying feet, several voices blending into one. I can't make out what they are saying. "25". " Officer Young".

I put Jayce down and sat beside him on the floor. Covering my ears trying to drown out the noise. I couldn't hear myself think. I looked at the boys and they were all crying. Crying for me. I closed my eyes and screamed.

I woke up in a sweaty panic. I sat straight up in bed. My breath was heavy and fast. I looked around the room. The sun was shining through the window and the clock read 6:45a.m. The kids were still asleep. I wiped my dripping forehead with the back of my shaking hand. These nightmares are so real lately. I got out of bed and went to the bathroom. I looked pale and my shirt had been drenched in sweat. I splashed my face with water and grabbed a new shirt from the dresser. I got dressed before the kids woke up and decided to write out some things that needed to be done. Phone calls that needed to be made.

The kids woke up around 7:15a.m. While they ate breakfast, I booked an appointment with the counsellor for Thursday. That's one item checked off the list. After breakfast, the playroom was opened so I let the boys go play while the Child and Youth Worker watched over them. I decided to take this time to help clean up the kitchen area and drink tea while I took down some more notes and filled out the housing application. That's another item off the list. I could see the boys from the table I was sitting at, the play room was right across from the kitchen area.

After the hour was up, I closed my book and went to get them. Jayce came running up to me like he hadn't seen me in hours.

"Mommy!" He gave me a big hug. Greyson and Bentley were still playing with some Lego and seemed happy to see me, but were still content and occupied with the Lego city they were working on.

Bentley picked up his towers to show me. "Look Mommy! Do you see what me and Greyson builded?" He was so proud.

Greyson stood up with Bentley. "Yeah, we made this tower a bank and there are apartments over here, some houses, and a jail. We made some guys to go in it and built a couch and beds for some of the houses."

I was pretty impressed that they were getting along so well and with the Lego city that they built. "Wow guys, that's pretty cool! I really like it"

Greyson grabbed on to my arm. "Mom, can we have a few more minutes to finish up our city?"

The worker came over to where we were. "Hey guys, I'll keep the room open an extra 15 minutes, but then we have to close up for a bit, okay?"

They jumped up and down with excitement, but with caution as they didn't want to drop their little city.

"There you go, guys. Make sure you say thank you!"

They said thank you as they placed their city down and continued working on it. Jayce had already run back to a play house where he had some babies wrapped in blankets. I walked around the room as they played. There were so many neat crafts hanging around the room and placed on the shelves. A lot of crafts I would love to do with the kids. There were some that I had seen on Pinterest before. I loved looking up crafts on there and doing them with the kids. I didn't always have the time or money for the supplies for some of the more elaborate crafts, but I tried. I loved the artwork we got to do together, it was something I have always loved doing.

I pulled my phone out to take a few pictures of the crafts I wanted to try with the kids. Then the Child and Youth Worker told the kids to start cleaning up.

"Alright guys, time to clean up our areas and head out with Mom. You guys can come back tomorrow and we can pull out some of the board games!"

Again, without a fuss or complaint, the boys all cleaned up their areas. I helped them clean up the Lego and put the babies back in the bin. I was impressed, who were these boys?

We got back to the room and picked up some of the laundry that needed to be washed. "Hey, since you guys have been so helpful lately, do you want to help Mommy with the laundry?"

Jayce was excited to help. "Mommy I help, I help." Jayce tried to pick up the basket but ended up toppling over with it.

"Thank you so much, Buddy. How about you help me put the clothes in the washer though and Mommy will carry the basket?"

Jayce stood up and nodded his head. Greyson offered to help carry the basket and Bentley carried the little bottle of laundry soap the women gave us when we first arrived. Laundry was put in and the room was clean. A movie was playing in the common room for the kids, so we decided to join in. It was SpongeBob and the boys were very fond of the silly shenanigans that SpongeBob and Patrick would get into.

After the movie finished, it was lunch time. The kids ate and wanted to play in the little play structure they had outside the shelter. It was chilly so we only stayed out for an hour before retreating back to the warmth. We then got washed up and ready for dinner, which was chicken noodle soup and egg salad sandwiches. The kids all ran to their favourite table, laughing about the entire way. When they all sat, another lady had been mumbling to herself and started speaking very loudly to the girl beside her. This was the same girl that was bothered when Jayce dropped his cup a few days ago.

"Fucking kids, like honestly, it's ridiculous."

Greyson looked at me, concern filled his face. "Mommy, are we going to get into trouble?"

I grabbed his hand. "No buddy, let's just try to be a little more quiet though because there are other people staying here too, right?" I felt bad, I knew his reaction was because of how things were at home. I had seen that scared look one too many times. The woman continued to mumble on rudely. I needed a positive way to deal with this. I wanted this to be a teaching lesson. I guess mostly for Greyson since the other two were still small. I didn't want to get pushed around, but I didn't want to kiss ass either, because then it wouldn't be any different than it was at home.

As I walked up to get the boys dinner, I stopped at the table where the woman was sitting. "Hey, I am sorry they can be a little loud, but they are kids. I will try to make sure they are a little more aware of everyone else around, but you kind of scared them. If we could find a way to meet in the middle, that would be great."

The lady didn't look as angry and nodded her head. "I haven't been able to sleep well and I am a bit grumpy. I am sorry." Better response than I was expecting.

"I understand that, I hope you can get some sleep soon." I continued towards the kitchen and grabbed the kids' dinner. I didn't want trouble with people in the shelter. We had to share this space for who knows how long. Maybe there was something I could do, like make everyone dinner. The food wasn't horrible here, but it wasn't exactly the best either. I would make a big salad, some chicken, and mashed potatoes with veggies. I know the kids would love to have some dinners they liked at home. I could pick up some things from the store tomorrow. Luckily, there was a Food Basics right across the street from the shelter.

I was excited to be able to cook for everyone. I am sure the shelter wouldn't mind. I should probably ask first. After the kids are done eating, I'll ask the woman at the front desk. I pulled out my notebook and began making a list of things I needed. I also had to check my bank account and make sure I had enough money. My HST payment had just come in, but I knew I would have to send half of that to you. I opened up my bank account on my phone and sent half the money to you. I also sent an email.

"We received HST. I sent half the money to your bank account."

There was a quick response.

"I don't understand how you can expect me to live with this little amount of money. I need to get things and this isn't enough money."

It's not exactly my problem anymore. You were one person and there were four of us in the shelter. I still sent you half which was $85. I thought that was more than enough to pick up some food for one person. When I left the house, there was plenty of food in the cupboards and still quite a bit in the fridge. I am in a shelter, but excuse me, I should have just sent you all of the fucking money and left the kids and myself with nothing. Not like we need anything at all. Not like you couldn't go out and get a job or ask someone for money if you really needed it, or maybe not spend all the money on junk food, electronics, and games constantly. Perhaps trying to not buy subscriptions for swingers apps and porn sites might help too.

I was furious and all it took was that little email. I wish I could reply and tell you exactly how I felt, but that came with consequences and it really didn't matter.

"I am sorry but I do need money as well. I have myself and the kids with me and you are a single person. I sent you half of what we got. I need to grab some things too."

Again, a quick reply.

"Thanks a lot. I guess I'll just starve, not that you give a shit."

Well, I am done with emailing today. Not even going to attempt to touch that one. I gave you half of what we got and I will not be guilted because of that. There is no reason why that couldn't get you groceries. You are no longer my concern or priority. The kids were my number one. I could have just kept all the money, but I didn't. Damned if I do, damned if I don't. You'll complain either way, again, it doesn't fucking matter what I do. I could have sent you all the money and you still would have found a way to complain. You won't take from these kids anymore; I won't allow it. Go ahead and complain, it's not going to work anymore.

I turned my focus back on planning the dinner. I also wanted to make up a mixture of some of my oils for the one lady. She mentioned she wasn't able to sleep so I thought I could make her something that could help. I always told the kids that acting mean to someone who was mean to you wasn't the right answer. Two wrongs don't make a right. This lady had been rude but I didn't know her or her situation. We were both in a shelter, it wasn't easy. I wanted to do something nice in the hope that it would smooth things over and make it a little easier on everyone.

I could have easily snapped back at her but I didn't want to, what good would it have done? It would have just created more tension and made things more difficult. I am just going to be positive and try to share some of that positively with others and go from there.

After dinner one of the ladies from the front desk approached us. "Hey Victoria, we can get a police escort to go to your home tomorrow for you to grab a few things. I know you wanted to grab some more of your things, right?"

Oh right! I had almost forgotten. "That would be great. Thank you so much!"

"Around noon is when the police will be coming. The kids can go in the play area with the Child and Youth Worker while you go."

I should probably make a list tonight of some of the things I need to grab. "Okay, that sounds great. Also, while you are here, do you think it would be okay if I made dinner tomorrow for everyone? I was going to pick up some things from the store."

She looked surprised. "Really? I am sure that the other ladies would absolutely love that!"

"I wanted to do something for everyone and the kids would like to have something they are used to eating, too."

"I think that's a great idea. That's very thoughtful of you."

I was really excited to be able to do something for everyone. I really think it's a good idea. Tomorrow was going to be busy, but good. I could finally grab my laptop and some more of our things, like clothes, toys, and books.

Next on the list was a phone call with Michelle. I knew that would be a lengthy phone call and we both had little ones. So, I planned to call after the kids were in bed. We headed back to our room after dinner and played superhero for 30 minutes before bath time, while we waited for your call. I was Commissioner Barbara Gordon and Jayce was Batman. Greyson and Bentley wanted to be Two Face and The Joker. The fight of good and evil stormed throughout the room. Blankets and pillows were thrown about in battle and clothes were scattered all around. I am not sure what part they played, but they were everywhere.

"Watch your step! Joker threw one of his silly gas bombs! Batman, use your grappler gun!" The battle was a long and rough one and the Commissioner was hurt pretty badly, but Batman saved the day! After, he needed a good bath to soak in all that glorious victory. A bath that was messy and loud with lots and lots of bubbles!

The kids were all clean and had their teeth brushed. It was past 7 and you never called or emailed. It was time for bed. I read them a book, kissed their little foreheads and chubby and dimpled cheeks and tucked them in, snug as a bug. I left their door open a crack so some light would shine in for Jayce, who was still a little afraid of the dark, and sat down on my bed and waited a few moments before making my phone call. I wanted to make sure they were sound asleep.

Once I could hear little snores from their room, I picked up my phone and dialed Michelle's number. The conversation was a long one. I told her everything. I told her that I was in a shelter and everything that you had done over the last several years. I told her how sorry I was about everything and she apologized too. We got Mom on the phone and caught her up as well. They wanted to come get me, but I told them it wasn't the right time. I needed to be here. They were helping me and I didn't know how everything was going to go. I was afraid leaving town was going to just feed into all the lies you had been telling. I needed to stay here for now. I had my family back and they understood. They had been waiting for the day that I called them. Mom began to cry.

"I just love you so much, Victoria. I didn't know what to do."

"I know, Mom. I didn't know what to do either."

We talked for hours. There were tears and there was laughter. It was exactly what I needed. I don't know why I was so afraid before. It's something I should have done a long time ago. Michelle told me all about Harmony and how sweet and funny she was. She does know about Aunty Victoria, which made me happy. Michelle showed her videos and pictures of when we were younger. She told Harmony all about her cousins and she even woke up during our phone call and I got to hear her little voice and talk with her. We made plans to get together since I was able to leave and go for a night or two. I told her I would message her and we could figure something out and get the cousins together.

After the phone call, I felt a lot better. Things really were going to be okay. We would eventually get out of here. We had family and support. Things weren't so bad. Something I dreaded and feared so much, coming to this shelter, ended up being a blessing in disguise. I was so very thankful.

I plugged my phone in and headed for the bathroom. I decided to take a quick shower, I was tired and didn't want to fall asleep in the bath. I washed my hair quickly and got out. I grabbed my pajamas from the dresser and fell into the bed to sleep. I played some soothing rainforest sounds on my phone before falling asleep. I listened to rain, rain forests, and waterfalls as they can help with nightmares and help with a more peaceful sleep. I loved the sound of rain. I closed my eyes as thunder quietly rumbled beneath the sound of rain droplets hitting the water and light noises from birds and animals. I felt myself slowly drifting into sleep.

29.

The kids were up at 5:35a.m. the next morning. Outside, the sky was still dark and there was a cold breeze that brushed the window and trees outside. I usually kept the window open a bit just to let some air in, but the cold air was a bit much today, so I closed the window above my bed and threw on a sweater. The room was dim and quiet. There were tired little giggles and whispers coming from the boys' room. I walked to the bathroom, picking up stuffed animals on the way. I switched the light on and got a glimpse of myself in the mirror again.

Normally I would try to avoid looking at myself, especially in the morning but for some reason, I noticed something different in my reflection. I couldn't really put my finger on it. I was clearly exhausted, which was evident because of the dark circles under my eyes and my hair needed a good combing, but I wasn't looking at myself thinking about how much weight I needed to lose or how ugly I was. I didn't see a damaged girl who was ready to give up. I saw something else, something familiar but why couldn't I figure it out?

"Mommy I have to pee." Bentley stood in the doorway, doing his little pee dance.

"Oh, sorry, buddy. Go pee."

He ran in singing, "Oh, I have to pee, I have to pee," until he reached the toilet and was able to pee. Then he started singing, "Oh I am peeing, Oh I am peeing."

Oh boy, these kids really crack me up. To be a child again, where your biggest concerns mostly involved food and toys and arguing over what pants you wanted to wear.

"Alright Benny, when you are finished, wash your hands and we can start getting ready to go out. You want to know where we are going?"

Bentley smirked and put his finger up in the air. "Hmmm, are we going to your butt?" This made him laugh hysterically.

"No, silly boy, we are not going to my butt. We are going to… McDonald's!"

Bentley's mouth opened and he squealed with excitement. Greyson then came running over.

"Um, did you just say McDonald's?"

I looked at Greyson and now Jayce who was behind him. "Yes, we are going to go to McDonald's for breakfast." I figured they could eat some breakfast and play at the play place for an hour or so before heading to the grocery store and grabbing some things for dinner. I also had to finish my list of things to grab from the house today to make sure I didn't forget anything.

I thought it would be a good idea to message you and let you know we were coming to grab some things. I didn't want to just show up and have you cause issues. Either way, there would be trouble, but it was worth a try.

"Sorry for the short notice, but last night I was informed I had a police escort to grab some of our things from the house. We will be coming around noon."

It was still pretty early so I didn't expect a quick reply this time. I did have a message from Michelle though.

"Hey, I am glad you reached out. It was nice talking again. Let me know when we can make some plans!"

Okay, so today is going to be a very busy day. Lots to do, lots to do. Need to get on it! Surprisingly, you did message back. Usually you were never up early so I honestly wasn't expecting it.

"I am busy, so no you are not coming to the house to get anything, you'll have to set up another day."

You would do anything to make things more difficult.

"Hey, I am sorry but I don't need permission to enter a house that I am on the lease for. It's not easy to get a police escort and this is the only time I am able to grab some of my belongings, so busy or not, I am coming to grab my things."

Maybe that had a little too much attitude? I don't know, it was too early to deal with this drama. I just knew that I didn't need permission to enter my own house and I needed some of the kids' things and my own. I finished getting the kids ready and didn't hear from you again.

The kids were very excited for pancakes and play time. I sat and drank my coffee and watched them play while I continued making my list of things to grab from the house. The kids needed some more of their clothes, as did I. I needed my laptop and some of the kids' favourite toys. They requested certain teddies and action figures along with some of their favourite books. I wanted to pick up some more of my oils as well, so I could make up some different mixes for the lady at the shelter. I knew I couldn't grab much, but little things that made the kids more comfortable would be great. I also wanted to grab some sentimental items that I was worried you were going to take or damage.

We left McDonalds around 10am and walked to the Food Basics across from the shelter. I grabbed everything I needed for dinner that night and headed back to the shelter to get ready for lunch and my trip back home.

The kids ate some macaroni and cheese for lunch and then made their way to the play area with the Child and Youth Worker. I knew I wasn't going far or for long, but I was a little nervous being away from them. I gave them a hug and kiss before I left and headed for the cruiser waiting outside. The lady at the front desk gave me three large garbage bags. That should be more than enough to grab what I needed.

I still hadn't heard from you again, so I wasn't sure if you would be there or not when we arrived. It gave my anxiety thinking about seeing you. The closer we got to the house, the more the anxiety rattled at me. The ride was quiet, only a few voices on the radio broke the silence every few minutes.

When we arrived at the house, the door was open, which meant that you were in fact home. I just needed to follow my list and get in and out as quickly as possible. The police officer was with me, so I was safe and didn't have to worry about arguments and name calling. The police officer was the first to go in. He knocked and opened the white screen door and gave a shout out before we came in.

Your voice came from the living room. "I'm here."

The officer motioned for me to go grab my things. He followed behind and stayed close. I grabbed most of the items from my room and the kids' room, but there were some things that I needed from the living room and the basement. When I walked down to the living room, you were sitting in your usual seat on the couch with your laptop open. You had the TV on in the background, as well.

I went to grab some of the kids' toys and my oils.

"You know that you didn't just buy them those toys, right? And they are going to need toys when they come back here to stay with me." I didn't want to say anything, so I continued to grab what I needed. "Also, those oils that you are taking, they are technically mine as well." I placed the items in the bag, continuing to ignore you. The last thing I needed was my laptop from the basement. "Yeah, thanks for ignoring me."

The anxiety had turned into irritation, every time you spoke. I knew that you were trying to bait me and get me into an argument, but I wasn't playing your game anymore. I needed my things and needed to get the hell out and away from you.

I grabbed my laptop from my desk in the basement. A screw was placed on the desk beside it. I checked the bottom and it was one of the screws for the laptop. I didn't have the tools to put it back in, so I just left it behind. I grabbed a few of my notebooks from my drawer and took a last glance at my desk to make sure I wasn't forgetting anything important.

I told the police officer that I had everything I needed and that we could go. You placed your laptop beside you and stood up to follow us out. Once out the door, you slammed it behind us and locked it. The task was done, I could go back to my boys and unpack our things. On the way back to the shelter I got a text message from Jeff.

"Hey! Did your friend get back to you by chance, about coffee?"

Oh right, I forgot to message back.

"Hey, Yes! She said she would do Wednesday at noon, if that works for you."

I didn't even know what we were going to talk about. I am sitting in a police car with garbage bags full of my things and heading back to the shelter I have been staying in with my kids. That's a great conversation starter.

"Yeah, actually that works great! I will see you then, Victoria."

I was excited to see him and get out for a coffee, I just didn't know how to go about the situation. Regardless, I'll have to figure it out and just go with the flow. Maybe leave out my current situation for now.

Back at the shelter, I placed the bags in our room before grabbing the boys. They were excited to get to play with their toys again while I put on the Pets movie. I folded clothes and placed them in the dressers we had and set up the kids' books and stuffies on the desk in their room. We kept busy until it was time to go out and make dinner. I already made a lavender concoction for the lady and had it placed in a little baggy.

Greyson and Bentley played while Jayce sat in a high chair beside me as I prepared dinner. Some of the ladies had walked by and noticed that I was the one cooking tonight. They were intrigued and excited for the meal.

The grumpy lady made her way out about 10 minutes before dinner was ready. She sat at her usual table with a newspaper. I walked over and placed the oil beside her on the table

"Hey, I hope you don't mind, but you mentioned that you are having trouble sleeping, so I just made this lavender mix of essential oils for you. You could rub it on your neck and chest before bed."

She looked up from her paper. Her unwelcoming facial expression softened up a bit. "That was really kind of you, thank you so much." She looked over at the kitchen and back at me. "Are you making everyone dinner tonight?"

"Yes, I picked up some things for my favourite salad and I am making some chicken, mashed potatoes, and veggies."

She looked surprised and her face was now gentle and kind. "Wow, that's really nice of you to do, I am excited to try it. The food here is okay, but it will be nice to have a good home cooked meal again. Thank you and I am sorry again for being short with the kids."

"That's okay. It's not easy being in a shelter and having to deal with what's on our plate. I get it."

She looked at me and nodded her head as she opened the lid to smell the oils. "This smells amazing and I will be using it tonight before bed."

The timer for the chicken had gone off so I scurried back into the kitchen.

I made plates for the boys and watched the women come up with their looks of excitement before grabbing some food. I made a plate for the ladies at the front desk as well. Everyone had thanked me for such a delicious meal and it felt good to help out and bring even a little bit of joy to other people. I didn't know their story or why they were here, but if I could somehow impact their lives while I was here and make it better for them, then I would.

After dinner, the other women offered to clean up since I had cooked. I wasn't going to refuse some help! I swept up the floors and cleaned the tables while the others washed dishes and mopped the floor. It was getting late by the time we got back to our room, so I bathed all the boys and settled down with a movie until 7:00, when you would be calling.

Again, the conversation didn't go well. I knew you were angry with the pick up today and it showed during the phone call. Every phone call, so far, had been stressful. You had also missed some nights. The times you did call though, the conversation never went smoothly. I thought you would have a little empathy for the kids and the situation they were in; show them a little understanding and compassion. Bentley is afraid to speak to you, it doesn't help when you raise your voice or give him a rude tone on the phone. Your voice triggers him and sets him off. It's beyond heartbreaking to see how scared he is to even say hello to you. I really try hard to prepare them for the phone call and to encourage them to say hi, good night, and that they love you. I would tell them how much you loved them and missed them. Nothing I said could change the actions they saw from you.

The phone calls would stress me out as well. I started breaking out in hives and every time I heard your voice on the other end. It was like a knife was being lodged into my chest. Bentley would be tense and begin tearing up even before the phone rang. It was a mess. Since the first phone call at Sharon's, I should have known that it wouldn't get better.

Greyson was the oldest, but not yours. Even though you didn't speak to him, the phone calls affected him, as well. He harboured a lot of anger towards you for how you treated me and how you treated him and his brothers. Even though he didn't want to talk to you, he was angry that you never even asked or thought about him. As soon as we left that house, Greyson was dead to you. I don't know what he was before, more of a nuisance to you than anything, but it was clear that being in his life since he was a toddler, meant absolutely nothing to you. Bentley, still young, picked up on your treatment of Greyson and he would constantly ask why he wasn't treated the same way as him and Jayce. Kids know more than we like to admit, they see more than we think, and it's soul crushing to know how much they had seen and picked up on.

The entire few minutes of being on the phone with you was like living with you all over again. Making sure they sat completely still not making any other noises but speaking to you. Every phone call leads to baiting and you trying to argue or blame me for something.

Every phone call also resulted in an email stating that I was interrupting the phone call and purposely distracting them so that they wouldn't speak with you. It was stressful and hard on all of us. The kids felt the pain I did. You didn't only abuse me, I wish it was only me, but you abused and damaged them. That's what hurt me the most out of anything that had happened so far. I wouldn't have cared as much if the abuse was just towards me. I am a grown up, I can handle it, and eventually get over it, but you were so cruel to those children. It hurt me every time and I tried speaking up, but every time it started a huge argument that would only end with me apologizing and correcting my poor behaviour. I was weak and needed to learn how to parent better. My job was to back you up and support you in your decisions towards the children. It wasn't right. None of it.

After the phone call, I received that expected email.

"Do you know what parental alienation is? It's what you are doing right now with the kids. Parental alienation is child abuse and you are abusing the children through this. I feel sorry for the kids and that they have to live with someone as selfish as you. You refuse to let me speak to my sons and are constantly talking over us. Purposely trying to distract them while trying to instigate arguments with me and bait me, so you can get something to use against me. Remember karma is a royal bitch and there will be consequences for your actions. You're not invincible."

I never knew how to respond to your emails. I knew that all you were doing was trying to upset me and get me going. It's so hard to just sit back and keep my cool. All I wanted to do was implode. I hated when you lied and twisted things around and tried to manipulate situations. I started making it a habit to record the phone calls because I couldn't take it anymore. I emailed you and told you to stop with the lies because I was recording the phone calls now and all it got was a cocky reply.

"You make me laugh, you don't think that I too have the ability to record phone calls? Frankly I don't give a fuck what you are doing…"

And on it goes. I tried to let go of the hateful rage that I held inside, but it was becoming more and more difficult. It made me sick. I was angry and furious that you had taken my story and twisted it so horribly into this mutated monstrosity and you made it your own. You turned my story into one about you and how you were the abused one and made yourself out to be the poor victim in it all. You made me the villain of my own story before I could even admit to myself that I was a victim.

I was isolated as friends and family were pushed away. I made the mistake of protecting and lying for you. I knew it was wrong, but I was supposed to support and side with you because you were my partner. We are no longer partners and you couldn't control me anymore. I had my family back. I talked to Michelle and Mom and it went better than I ever could have imagined. They weren't mad at me and they didn't hate me like you said they did. I sent them messages from you and they read them all. They knew who you were now. They had seen it before but I confirmed it.

Michelle was going to take some time off and come down with Mom in the next week. We were all going to stay at a hotel for a night or two and they were going to help me figure some things out.

With everything going on, even with the stress, things seemed to be looking up and getting better. I had to start thinking about switching the kids' school though, and I needed to hand in the housing application. I needed to let go of the small hope of returning home and having the kids stay in the same school. I needed to let go and move forward.

30.

Two weeks had passed and the kids were ready to start at their new school in a few days. We transferred their files and even got an email on a small apartment. Michelle was going to come down with Mom to look at it with us. I was told to make a list of things that I would need in order to move and to see if I was able to retrieve any more items from home. The shelter said they would help with what they could, but they couldn't help with everything. I sent an email out to you.

"I have begun a search for a new place for the kids and me. I need to know everything that I will need for our place, so if we could please have a civil conversation about the items in the house and if we could divide some of them, that would be greatly appreciated."

It only took you 2 minutes to reply.

"Don't bother, my parents said they would help me find an apartment. I won't be here next week, so the house is yours."

Wait, what? I had to read the email a few times over to try and process the content. Next week? The kids and I can go home next week. We won't be homeless and living in a shelter, we can go back home to our neighbourhood, the kids can go back to their school, and sleep in their own beds. We can go back home. Next week we are going back home.

I was dumbfounded. You showed absolutely no interest in leaving the house and had been completely unreasonable and difficult to deal with up to this point and now you were leaving the house? I called Sharon and told her the news. I called Michelle and Mom and informed the ladies at the front desk. There were a few things we needed to do before I was allowed to go back home, like calling the landlord to have the lease and locks changed after you had left. They wanted to make sure the kids and I would be safe going back and there would no longer be disputes over who had to leave or not. The house would be mine and in my name. I couldn't understand why all of a sudden you decided to be the one to move, but my excitement over shadowed the doubt and worry that swam in the back of my mind.

I slowly started to feel more comfortable with the fact that things wouldn't always be bad. I knew that there was still a long road ahead of us, but things certainly didn't seem so dark anymore. The week went by without a hitch. I had a counselling session Thursday and the day before I went out to coffee with Jeff. The first date went surprisingly well. Most of the conversation was about hobbies and career aspirations, which got my thinking of what I wanted to do when we got back home. Michelle and Mom were going to come down and help me get back home with all of our things and stay the first night, so we weren't alone.

When the day came, it was bitter sweet. It was almost surreal. We stayed in a shelter for the last few weeks and it wasn't as bad as I thought it would have been. I didn't make friends while we were here, but I definitely built a bond with some of the ladies and the Child and Youth Worker. I didn't want to say that I would miss it, but I would miss it. This place helped save my children and me. This was home for the last few weeks and I don't know where we would have ended up if it wasn't for the shelter and the staff here. This was the start to our new journey and I will always be grateful for it. I was excited to get back to our old routine; a new old routine. I was excited to be able to create it with the kids and have more dance parties and have the kids friends over more and explore being our own little family in our home. I was also a little nervous about what we would be walking into. I didn't know the state of the house, what things would be missing or broken. I didn't know how I would feel stepping back into the house where so many bad memories lived.

Once Michelle, Mom, and I walked in with the kids, it was much like when I had first left. At first glance there wasn't much that was different. Your things were no longer all around the house. Your electronics, books, and clothes had all been taken. Dirty dishes piled in the sink and the fridge had been empty. You had switched up the rooms and I noticed some of the kids' items were gone. I wasn't going to worry about taking inventory of all the missing items just yet. It was late and I had other things to focus on like getting the kids ready for bed and getting our things unpacked.

One thing that I hadn't anticipated was the feeling that hit me once the hype was gone and the house had settled. It all had hit me. The first night back in the house. I thought about everything that we had overcome to get to this point and everything that happened. All the hurt and struggle and what was to come. It was all so real, everything that happened. It was no longer a secret I had to keep. Everyone knew.

As everyone slept, I sat up wide awake. Unable to settle my thoughts, I decided to look around and assess the damage. I noticed some of my clothes and notebooks missing. I knew how vindictive you were, so it was to be expected. I already knew my items would be broken or missing but I noticed some of the children's favourite toys were missing and some of their sentimental baby items were gone. The only reason for you to take something like that was to hurt me. You never cared much about sentimental value. Their drawings or paintings they handed you, you always wanted to throw them in the garbage. You didn't care to keep things like their first haircut or first tooth. In fact, you often threw a fit and we argued constantly over me keeping the kids' things.

"You can't keep everything they draw, Victoria. It's a waste of space and there's no reason to keep it. Victoria, you need to get rid of this crap, are we going to be using any of it?

No. You have a serious problem, you think everything is sentimental, you need to grow up and organize your shit and get rid of things".

It was a constant battle over things I wanted to keep. I had a bin for each kid with some of their baby clothes and a favourite baby toy, a small cabinet filled with school and art work from them, and the occasional special rock they collected while we were out and about on trails. Heck yes, I kept that stuff. When we were at home and making crafts and all Bentley could do at the time was a few scribbles, I would put his name and the date on it and file it away in the cabinet. I have always been sentimental with love letters, baby books, and certain objects found on adventures. I didn't see anything wrong with that. You can look back on that memory and when the kids were all grown up and have their own kids, they could have that stuff to show their kids or grandkids. They could show off that special rock from the day we went to the beach. Bentley had learned how to swim on his own that day and he got sand stuck in his butt crack. This was just one of the silly and funny stories we could cherish together.

When I had noticed some of these items missing, I felt heartbroken. Those are things I can't replace. I could replace some of my clothes and whatever else you broke and took that belonged to me, but the kids' things, I couldn't get back. The hat Jayce came home in from the hospital or the special pictures they drew when they were little. You didn't care about any of it, so where did it go, the garbage? I felt sad but anger quickly replaced that feeling. I know it would be a bad idea but I sent you a message anyway. I was in such an emotionally messed up place and I just was furious that you just couldn't stop. It was one thing after another.

"I don't understand why you would take some of the kids' sentimental things and break my things, but I would like them back. You never cared about that stuff and it's important to me and you know that. I have tried being civil with you and helping you and you just keep trying to tear me down. I want the things back."

I paced back and forth in the living room with my phone close to my face. Waiting for the reply. It took about 15 minutes before my phone dinged.

"I have no idea what you are talking about. I don't have any of your stuff and I have no reason to break your things. I documented the entire house and everything I had left there, which was quite a bit. Thousands of dollars worth of things actually. You could have broken things and are now trying to frame me. Just like you did when you told the police officers that I pushed you into the wall and how you took pictures of the bins that fell on the floor and said I threw them at you. This is further proof that you have no interest in getting along. Stop living in your illusion and fantasy world, Miss poor, little victim. Leave me alone about your stuff. Bye."

My entire body began to shake. I don't know if it was the anger, intense frustration or sadness, but I couldn't stop shaking. I was so sick and tired of how much you lied and tried to play Mister nice guy and the innocent one. You twisted our entire life and tried to make it seem like you were the abused one and I did everything to you. Every damn word that came out of your mouth was injected with poison. Your lying really got to me and you knew that.

I continued to pace angrily in the living room talking to myself. I threw my phone on the couch and rubbed my head. You know you shoved me into the wall while I was holding our infant son and you completely disregarded his safety. I couldn't believe how vindictive you were, especially coming from someone who cheated and abused everyone he lived with! YOU cheated, YOU wanted out of the relationship, and YOU abused not only me, but the kids as well! I am the bad person for speaking up about it. You didn't like that you lost control of me and I told on you. You hated that people found out about what you were doing. You hated that people found out about the real you.

I held back tears. If I told you any of this, it would trigger more fighting and arguing and it really wasn't worth it. You knew the truth, you were caught in lies with the police and everyone else and you just couldn't handle people seeing the real you.

I used to look for your approval, I begged for it. I did everything you asked and tried so fucking hard to make you proud of me, for you to respect and love me. I don't know why I tried so damn hard. I don't know why I missed and ignored all the red flags and signs. You were never really that nice to me, you always talked down to me, and you always made me feel stupid. Why the hell did I want your approval so badly? Even after the first night you became physical with me and you left for a few days, I missed you and believed things would be okay and that we could make things work. You told me that your family treated you horribly and made me feel bad for you. How could you miss someone who treated you that terribly? I grew to dislike you and not want to be near you. You made me hate myself. I wanted to be away from you, but at the same time, I wanted to make you happy. It's like it was my life's mission to make you happy and just get that "I love you" and "I am so proud of you" from you. Anything that showed me that you appreciated me, even just a little. I never got that approval from you.

I would try to think about any good times that we had, which were very few. I thought if it could be good sometimes, then there has to be something there, even if it was only once every few months, there was some light. So why couldn't it be like that everyday? It made me wonder what the motive was behind every hug and every kiss. At the time, I thought it was love but when you wrapped your arms around me, were you just holding a knife to my back?

The more I thought about the good times between us, I realized that you were intoxicated, every time. Through all the memories, I couldn't find one where we had a genuinely connecting sober moment. There was not one that meant something special. I really tried to understand you. I believed that you were good and just someone who had been hurt and needed to be shown love and compassion. I didn't really know who you were. I didn't realize the evil that laid dormant, the evil that patiently waited to awaken at the right time, and the evil that tried to destroy me.

For a long time, I prayed for things to go back to the way they were when we first started dating but then I realized, that wasn't real. Going back would be going back to ignoring the signs, going back to darkness, lies, and secrets. Things weren't okay. I was just oblivious to what was going on and ignored the obvious red flags that many tried to warn me about. There was no going back with you and there was no future with you either. There was no respect, no loyalty, and no love. You knew all the right things to say. You took my heart, my weakness, and manipulated it to get your way and for that, you are at fault. However, I will always blame myself for staying too long after realizing the truth. I will forever blame myself for enabling you and allowing you to do what you did, for lying, abusing and hurting, and for defending you when you were in the wrong because it was what good girlfriends were supposed to do. I now know right from wrong and it was all wrong. It was all wrong.

31.

The next morning, I tried to stay positive. I had what truly mattered, my children. I was keeping them safe and that was everything to me. I was so happy the kids got to meet their cousin and played all day long. We took the kids to the park to play and even went to the butterfly conservatory. The kids all had a blast. Michelle and Mom were reluctant to leave that night, but Michelle had work the next day and had to get back home with Harmony. Mom also had some appointments she had to tend to and it wouldn't be long before we took a visit back home.

After just a few weeks, there were massive changes in the children's behaviour and their confidence. Even just the first few days of being away from you, you could see changes in them. Bentley had been improving at school tremendously and the teachers had been commenting on him smiling more in school since he had been back. They mentioned how he seemed to be enjoying activities more and interacting with other kids.

Everyone immediately saw a difference in all the children after you had left. They saw them being children for the first time. It was incredibly hard, but here we are. I had so much to be grateful for and so much to be happy about and it all stems from these boys. I kept this in mind through all the text messages, through the lies and manipulation. I try to keep this in mind through all the hateful words and emotional abuse because I know that I can make it; I am strong enough to fight through it and come out on top.

Once I had seen the kids doing so well and adjusting to the new routine, I decided to take Jeff up on his offer for a movie night out. We had been talking on and off for the last few weeks and I felt more comfortable and stable enough to just see how things would progress, go on a date or two, and continue talking. Regardless of the stress you poured into my life, things were going fairly well and getting back on track. Sharon had already mentioned about babysitting the kids while we went out for a movie, so I messaged her and set up a date.

I sent Jeff the confirmation text and butterflies were fluttering around in my belly as I hit the send button. I was still a little nervous about going on a date, but I was also excited and eager. I was looking forward to relaxing and having a fun night out. Maybe cuddling in the movie theatre and Jeff trying the old yawn and placing his arm around me. I couldn't wait for Friday night. I had two days of waiting and wondering and trying to imagine how the night will be. Until then though, it's Mom duty.

32.

On Friday, Sharon arrived a little early for some catch up time and a coffee. We let the kids play outside until I left around 7:00 to meet for 7:30. I arrived at Jeff's about five minutes early. I was still a little nervous about meeting at his house, but I was so excited to be able to relax, maybe get in some cuddles, and possibly a PG 13 make out session. The door of the red bricked duplex opened. Jeff was standing on the other side of the door, dressed in a black t-shirt and dark blue jeans. He smiled.

"Hey beautiful lady, why don't you take a step into the house of Jeff and I'll give ya a small tour?"

I walked into the house and took my shoes off and placed them on the shoe rack beside the hall closet. He led me down the hall to this quaint little kitchen, then to the bathroom, living room and finally his bedroom. The walls were decorated in paintings and pictures of family and friends. The paintings were of night skies, thick green forests and beautiful waterfalls and ponds. "I love the paintings you have, they are so beautiful."

Jeff stopped in front of the painting of the city at night, the buildings and lights reflecting off the water. "This is my favorite right here. I love going into the city at night. The beautiful sights in New York, I tell ya."

"Oh, you have been to New York?"

Jeff smiled again. " Oh yeah, I have been all over, I must say though, New York is in my top three favourites." Jeff took my hand. "Here, come to the living room so we can get comfy on the couch and pick out a movie." He led me back to the living room and took a seat on the couch. The room was dark, the only light was the light emulating from the TV screen. Jeff moved closer to me and crossed his legs as he slowly put his arm around me. In his left hand, he held a black TV remote. "Any ideas on which movie you would like to watch?"

I felt nervous as his hand caressed my shoulder but his hand felt warm and soft on my bare skin. "Oh, I am good with anything, really."

Jeff looked at me and smiled again, only this smile made me feel a little off. The blue light from the TV cast a creepy shadow over his face. "Oh yeah? That's good to know." He lightly squeezed my arm as he said this, which gave me an uneasy feeling in my gut. I think maybe I led him on a little too much. Maybe coming here for our first date was a mistake. He continued, "Here, how about we watch 16 candles, every girl likes that movie?"

I nodded my head and smiled. I actually loved that movie. "Yeah, I am good with that."

Jeff played the movie and moved his hand from my shoulder. He brought his arm around as he stretched and readjusted his body. He then placed his hand above my knee on my thigh and slowly moved his hand up and down. Getting higher each time his hand came back up. "I am really glad you came over for a movie, I really like you." His smile seemed sincere but there was something unsettling in his tone.

I nodded again. "Yeah, me too, you seem like a really nice guy." We had a good time on the coffee date, we laughed and joked the entire time. He was a complete gentleman, he didn't even try to kiss me before parting ways. He gave me a tap on the shoulder and gave me a "See ya later". I felt his hand rubbing higher now.

"I, um-" I tried closing my legs together, but Jeff's other hand swung around and stopped my right leg from moving.

"It's okay, don't be nervous. I'll be gentle."

"I just, I don't think we should just because we still don't know each other that well. I just want to take things slow is all."

Jeff chuckled a little. "Who says we need to know each other better?" His words now matched his tone.

I felt his lips on my neck as his hand rubbed harder on the outside of my pants. I felt my chest tighten. "Jeff, I am sorry but I don't-"

He placed his hand firmly on my shoulder and pushed me back. Forcing me to lay down on the couch. He was quickly on top of me. Grinding against me hard while suffocating me with his kiss. I couldn't speak. I didn't want to be here anymore. I wanted to leave. I tried to push his torso up and off of me, but he grabbed my wrists and pinned them down to my sides.

"What's wrong? Your ex said you were easy, but you seem to be resisting a lot. You're a horny, bad girl aren't you, Victoria? We both know why you came here tonight and it wasn't to watch a movie."

My heart sank into my stomach. "Wait, excuse me? My ex? I, I want up. I don't know what you are talking about. Please just get off of me." I tried to get up again and was pushed back down with more force. His grip around my wrists became tighter. "Jeff you are hurting me."

Jeff placed his hand over my mouth. "Shut the fuck up, you little tease." He continued to grind against me while softly moaning. He let go of my wrist and began unbuckling his pants. I tried using both hands to pry his off of my mouth, but he only squeezed harder. Soon, his free hand was sliding down my pants. I tried to scream. I tried to hit him but the pain of him squeezing my face with his nails became too much. "Shut up. If you scream, I'll fucking kill you."

The fear in my eyes confirmed to Jeff that I understood, he knew I wasn't going to scream. He let go of my mouth and began sliding my pants off.

"Please, please stop. I don't want to do this, just let me go home and I swear I won't tell anyone. I won't say anything to anyone ever."

His hands moved up my trembling legs, spreading them and moving in between them. He came close enough to whisper in my ear. I felt his hot breath on my neck. "You're a dirty little slut and you know you want this. You're going to fucking take it and like it." He pushed himself into me hard and fast. It hurt and it didn't stop hurting. The tears came down and they didn't stop either. "You fucking love that, don't you?"

I continued to plead with him to please stop, that it was hurting and I swore I wouldn't tell anyone. I didn't want this. I wanted to be home. This was a mistake and I should never have come here. This was all my fault. I should have kept walking and ignored him that day. I shouldn't have been thinking about boys, especially at a time like this. I felt him bite and scratch my neck and chest and with every thrust, the excruciating pain surged.

I stopped fighting. It was a lost cause at this point. The more I fought and the more tense my body was, the more it hurt. I tried to relax my body the best I could and tried to clear my mind and go somewhere else. Anywhere else, I didn't care where, just as long as I wasn't here, lying on this couch, faint noises in the background from the forgotten movie playing, and the loud moaning and heavy breathing coming from Jeff. I took my mind somewhere that I often went, to the dreams for the future, of what could be. I often saw the kids playing in the yard of a little family home. They would be running around with puppies and friends and I would have the love of my life sitting next to me, enjoying coffee and the children's laughter together on our porch. We would spend summer nights out in the back playing games and having fires where we would roast marshmallows and hot dogs while enjoying the stars above. We would take day trips to the zoo or the water park and at the end of the day, take the kids to Dairy Queen for an ice cream cone. After the kids were all settled in bed, the hubby and I would cuddle up to a movie and fall asleep in each other's arms, exhausted from the day, but happy and full of love. I desperately wanted this, I thought about it often. I dreamt and wished for a life like this.

A sharp pain pulled me from my thoughts. My cheek now stung, that familiar pain.

"Fuck," Jeff moaned as he took in a long breath and thrust hard and deep inside me one more time before pulling away and sitting on the other side of the couch. His hand wrapped around himself and he finished on his black t-shirt. "He was right about how tight you were."

My legs trembled as I closed them together. I sat up and began scanning the dark room for my pants. Once I found them, I reached out to grab them. I was stopped when Jeff grabbed my wrists tightly, pulling me over to him and using my arm to guide me down to my knees in front of him. His free hand grabbed the back of my head and filled his hand with my hair. He pulled my face closer to his.

"You made a mess, It's only polite to clean it up." His hand then forced my head down as he thrusted inside of my mouth. The taste was bitter. "Just like that."

The thought of biting it off crossed my mind for a moment but I thought against the idea. I don't think I could ever actually bite hard enough and would probably just end up making him angry. Jeff pulled me up, my hair still in his hand, gave me a hard kiss on the lips, and pulled me back to look into my eyes. He wiped the tears and running mascara off with his thumb and combed my hair with his fingers. His rough touch became soft again.

"Now get the fuck out of here and if you tell anyone about tonight, you'll be sorry."

"I understand." I picked up my pants and slid them on while Jeff stood up and buckled his pants. As he was taking his shirt off, I walked to the hall and grabbed my shoes. I didn't look back and I didn't bother to slide my shoes on before leaving the house. The streets were empty and the air was chilly. No car or person in sight. Just the street lights above. I felt sick and dizzy. I didn't want to go home, but I didn't know where I wanted to go. To the police station? No, there would be consequences I knew that already. How could you do this to me, what did you tell Jeff in order for him to agree to something like this? Unless, he's just like you. He would have to be just like you to do what he did. I remember you mentioning a friend from counselling, but I never remembered his name. You had mentioned it months ago. I thought it was good for you to make friends, but to my knowledge, you didn't talk often or want to hang out with them when I told you that you should. Maybe all the library trips and walks weren't always going to meet other women, but Jeff too.

I thought things couldn't get worse from here. You had already done so much, how could it possibly have gotten worse? I knew you had this darkness inside your soul, or whatever it was that was there. I knew you were a monster, but I had never thought you would be capable of something like this.

When I got home I walked up to the bathroom. The kids and Sharon were sleeping. I wanted to wash him off of me; I could still smell his cologne as if he was standing right beside me. I undressed slowly because I was so sore. I looked in the mirror and saw bruises and scratch marks on my wrists and chest. I pulled my pants down and noticed there was blood. Fresh tears fell as I climbed into the bath and turned the water on.

33.

I stayed up most of that night thinking. Things needed to change and I still had so much to do. I was out but still stuck in this vicious cycle. I needed to be away from you for good. You weren't going to stop. Not until I was dead. I underestimated what you were capable of, I know that now. I got up early before everyone woke up and began making breakfast. I didn't want to think about what happened and wanted to move on. I brewed some coffee and got some pancakes and eggs going. I heard little footsteps and knew that one of the kids had woken up. Greyson came into the kitchen to grab something to drink.

"Good morning, Greyson."

Still rubbing his eyes he looked up at me. "Good morning, Mommy"

"Did you have a good night last night with Sharon and your brothers?"

"Yeah, we went to the park and I fell but I was okay. We watched Superman and had some treats. It was fun!" He had such a big smile on his face.

"I'm glad you guys had fun! I am just making some breakfast, why don't you go turn on some cartoons and I'll call you up when it's done?" Greyson nodded his head, grabbed some water and headed down stairs. Bentley and Jayce joined Greyson a few minutes later, running down the stairs into the living room. Sharon came down next, yawning and stretching. She walked towards me with a very mischievous smile and nudged my side.

"Heyyyyyyyy, so how did it go?"

I rehearsed it like 20 times last night, what I was going to tell her, but trying to get the words out proved to be more difficult than I had anticipated. "It was okay, I just don't think I am too interested in him."

Her smile faded. "Awe, really? What Happened?"

I casually shrugged my shoulders. "Nothing really, I just wasn't feeling it, you know? Guess I am just not ready to get back out there yet."

Sharon patted my shoulder a few times. "Well, that's alright. No need to rush, right? At least you put yourself out there and you tried. Now and know for sure you need more time."

I smiled and nodded and finished cooking breakfast.

"Thanks for watching the kids for me, by the way."

"Oh, no problem, they were awesome! I am going to get going now though, sorry I couldn't stay longer. Have to go pick up my babies." Sharon gave me a hug and headed for the door.

"Do you want a pancake for the road?"

"Sure, I'll take one."

I passed her a plate of pancakes and waved as she headed out the door. "Text me later, Sharon!"

"Will do!"

The door shut and I called the kids up for breakfast. I listened to them hustle up the stairs. Some days they sounded like a herd of elephants running around the house. They were crazy little guys but it made me smile. I really appreciated their craziness, especially today. Even with my emotions all over the place the last while, those boys could always make me smile. Some days they would drive me nuts, give me headaches, drive me up the wall, and not let me rest or recoup from their wild ways, but honestly, I wouldn't trade it for all the calmness in the world. Not a damn chance. I love seeing them enjoy life to the fullest; not a care in the world just living in the moment and enjoying every second of it.

The rest of the day went by quickly. We went to the park and played, we got ice cream, dealt with little tantrums and little fights over toys, had a bath, and cuddled to the Spiderman movie until they all fell asleep. I carried them all to bed and cleaned up the day's fun and excitement. Dishes, floors, and laundry that consisted of grass stained pants and shirts from the boys rolling down the hill for an hour. I went to bed, feeling thankful for the day and didn't think of Jeff until I laid in bed and felt how sore my body was. I didn't cry. I refused to cry. Instead, I rolled to my side, closed my eyes and thought about the future.

34.

7:30 a.m my phone dinged. The house was silent, which meant the kids were still asleep. I wiped my eyes and glanced at my phone. It was an email from you. What the hell could you possibly want this early in the morning? Then, the night with Jeff crossed my mind. I felt a rage building up inside me. I felt disgusted and bitter. It was you who set it up. I still couldn't wrap my head around it, but I didn't want to think about it. I could try for years to understand your mentality, the way you think, and who you are, but I wouldn't be able to. Honestly, I don't think I ever want to understand either. I opened the message knowing it would probably have something to do with Jeff.

"I was informed that you were leaving the children with someone you didn't know just so you could go out and sleep around, like you have been for years. If this type of behaviour continues, I will have to inform Children's Services so that the children can be in the care of someone who will take care of them properly and not leave them with strangers to go sleep with random people. That is completely irresponsible on your part and you should know better. Your children should come first, but I know that's too much to ask for considering how much of a selfish narcissist you are. You have been warned."

What. The. Actual. Fuck. I sat up in bed and pulled my arm back behind my head. I took a moment, thought about what I was about to do and decided fuck it. I threw my phone across the room with every ounce of strength I had. I heard my case crack as it hit the wall followed by a thud as it hit the ground in pieces. I picked up my pillow and screamed into it, muffling my screaming and swearing. After a minute, I put the pillow down and crept downstairs to check on the boys. I was hoping my phone hitting the wall didn't wake them up. When I got downstairs, they were all still sleeping. Usually at night, they were heavy sleepers but closer to the morning, even a creek on the floor would wake them up. I didn't want them waking up to me being upset or angry. I didn't want them seeing me like that. They had seen enough of that while you were here. They needed the Mom I was before I met you and the Mom you tried to break. I'm still here though. I fought tooth and nail to keep those parts of me intact. I was angry, I was sick, and I was hurt but I wasn't going to let it take me down. Not after everything we have been through; what you put us through. I have to stay strong.

I tiptoed back upstairs and picked up the pieces of my phone. The phone was actually only cracked slightly. I opened the email again. I hit reply, typed in DO NOT EMAIL ME AGAIN, and hit send. I turned off the notifications for the app. You will not break me.

35.

The weeks following the incident with Jeff, you made sure to keep your promise from the day I left for the shelter. That you would make my life miserable. I continued to fight off your accusations and try to stay positive for the kids. You made up outrageous lies about me and our life together. You fabricated stories about our relationship, how we lived together, arguments, and incidences. You wouldn't stop with the mind games with the police, your family, and Children's Aid. You continue to get away with everything. Threats, false accusations, all of it. In one email, you blamed me for being in the shelter with the kids. You said it was my fault and that I failed them and scarred them. You said I am doing a good job at playing the victim, that I am abusive, a drug addict, and that the kids are not safe with me. You constantly threatened to have them taken away from me. You didn't care if they went into foster care or were thrown in the system, you just wanted to hurt me.

I had been trying to speak out, but all the years of me lying for you and hiding the abuse, had been used against me. I never told anyone how bad things had been or how you treated the kids and me. When others had seen it, I defended you. I gave excuses and tried to justify what you were doing. No one believed me when I finally spoke up. I understood why because I had put myself in that position. I should have said something sooner. I should have told someone when it was happening. I was scared and ashamed and by the time I wanted to say something, I was too deep in the pool of lies and abuse. I couldn't see a way out. Only to continue going deeper and deeper, until I finally drowned.

Through all of this, I stayed strong. I kept thinking about the kids. They were what mattered. I needed to keep fighting. I knew if I stayed on course, I continued to work towards the future and push through all of this madness, I could make it. I was fucking doing it. Until the day something happened that would throw me off this careful constructed course.

I had taken the kids to school. Jayce and I had spent the day at his favourite park. I was messaging Sharon and making plans for a movie sleepover. I spent most of my day running around the slide with Jayce and had a small picnic under the willow tree beside the park. Jayce had enjoyed some raspberries and a sandwich while I sipped at some coffee.

When it was time to pick up the kids, Jayce and I left the park 20 minutes before. The park was about 10 minutes down the street from the school, which left us with plenty of time to get there. Once we got to the school, I let Jayce play in the sandbox while we waited for the bell. My phone was vibrating in my back pocket like crazy. I thought maybe I was getting a phone call. When I pulled the phone out of my pocket, I looked at the screen and had seen several messages from different people and two missed phone calls. I usually don't get too many messages or phone calls, especially all at once. I felt a little worried and uneasy about all the messages. Had something happened to someone I knew? I opened up one of the messages from an old friend from high school. There was a photo attached to the message. The message read, "Hey Victoria, I just received this, is this you?"

I opened the photo. I instantly couldn't breath. My chest felt like it had collapsed. The photo was me. It was an old photo taken months ago. I was standing in the bathroom mirror holding my white shirt up, bare breasts exposed and pink underwear. I took this photo, trying to make myself feel sexy and beautiful. I had always been self conscious. It was left on my computer when you stole my hard drive. This was the photo you followed me around the house with one day, shoving the screen in my face, calling me a whore. You threatened to send it to people before, to send it to anyone I tried to date. Now, I was looking at it on social media. You had created an entire Facebook page, added these photos, and sent a request to everyone on my friends list. I continued to get message after message. I couldn't respond to them all. I couldn't read them all. High school friends and teachers, old employers, family, everyone had seen this photo.

I looked up to check on Jayce and he was still playing in the sandbox. I had seen kids walking around but I didn't even notice the bell had rung. Greyson and Bentley were walking down the hill towards me. I felt numb and light headed. I felt like I was on autopilot. I wanted to scream, I wanted to yell and swear but over anything else, I wanted to throw up. My eyes stung, but I didn't want to cry, not here. Bentley reached me first, showing me a painting he did in class.

"Look Mommy, I painted this for you!" It was a tree with leaves and apples. There were four little people drawn around the tree.

"That is so cool, Buddy. I can't wait to hang it up on the fridge." I swallowed hard. Trying to contain my emotions. I picked up Jayce. We walked back home, but every step was a struggle. I tried to keep my breathing in check and tried to relieve the pressure against my lungs. Once we got into the house, I put a movie on and went up stairs to call Sharon. I tried to keep my emotions under control but once I started talking about it, I couldn't stop the tears. It was hard to breath. It was hard to talk. Sharon could barely understand me through my gasps and tears. I was breathing hard and fast. I knew I wasn't making much sense, but I couldn't do anything else. I couldn't think straight. She was already on her way to my house, so she told me to try and breathe, she will only be 10 minutes. I took that 10 minutes to try and calm myself. Splashing cold water on my face and breathing slowly. Sharon walked in while I was drying my face. I heard the front door and her footsteps coming up the stairs.

"What's going on, Victoria? I couldn't understand what you were saying on the phone, something about a picture?" I knew if I tried explaining it again, I would start crying. I just calmed myself down, so I gave her my phone.

"Oh my god! He fucking seriously did this? What the actual fuck?" She handed me the phone back and wrapped her arm around me tight. I could feel her body shaking and trembling with anger. She let go and started pacing. "What a fucking asshole. Why can't he just stop?" Sharon walked over to where I was standing and wrapped her arms around me tight again. I could feel her body shaking against mine, angry and just as upset as I was.

She let go and continued pacing. "You are the mother of his children and you were damn good to him. You did everything for him! You have tried to be civil and he just won't stop. You have to stand up and report this. Call the police. I am here with you and I'll help in any way I can."

Having Sharon here really helped calm me down. I felt my tense body loosening up and I had stopped crying. "I am tired of sitting back and letting him do all of this. I know I need to say something. I have to." The tears stopped. I tried to crack a smile at Sharon, trying to show that I was going to be okay. Then, there was a knock at the door. Sharon walked ahead of me so I had time to wipe my face. When she opened the door it was the social worker on our case.

"Hey Victoria, I don't mean to drop by unannounced but I received a phone call today from you know who, about you and your friend here."

This was maliciously done. You knew I would be vulnerable and upset from the photos you posted earlier.

"He called and expressed concern about the children's safety and that you and your friend were here doing drugs in front of the children. Now I know that this is far from the truth, but I have to follow up as it's part of my job. I have had several phone calls from him. I know you would never do those things and it's him trying to cause trouble."

I was so relieved she understood and that there would be no real trouble from his phone call.

She had noticed my red puffy eyes and looked at me with concern. "Are you okay? You seem a little upset."

Sharon knew I would start crying again if I started talking about the events from earlier, so she decided to explain to the worker what had happened.

She was disgusted. She advised me to call the police as soon as possible. She told me that everything was going to work out soon enough, to try and keep strong, and to keep fighting.

After she left, I took to social media to make a public apology to everyone that had seen the photo. Once the kids were sound asleep, Sharon and I called the police. During the phone call, I received a message from you, stating that if I didn't stop slandering you, you would have me charged. I was in disbelief. I knew you had been stalking all my profiles and social media, so I wasn't surprised you had seen the post. Although, I never used your name or said anything slanderous about you in my post, so you were just reaching and looking for anything to get at me.

I felt so ashamed and humiliated. I was embarrassed that everyone saw that photo. How was I going to deal with this? All I could think about was if there were more accounts out there. Instagram, more Facebook profiles, and whatever other websites you could get them on. How could you do that to me? I took care of you for years. I loved you and did everything for you. I was there for you when no one else was. I tried so damn hard to make things work, even after you had cheated the first and second time. And the time after that. I tried even after you became emotionally and physically abusive. Even after we broke up, I tried to be friends, to help you, and be there for you. It got too bad. I was so afraid for the kids' safety and I was afraid for my own.

You continue to try to tear me down. Bring me to my knees, begging for your forgiveness, begging you to please just stop, while you stand tall over me, smirking and basking in the power and control. I never knew someone so cruel in my life, not until I met you.

36.

The urges were gnawing at me worse than they had since that last night. I needed to relieve the pain and give in. I needed to give in now. The house was silent as the kids slept in their beds. Sharon left for an hour to go take care of something, so I was alone. I took this chance to walk into the kitchen and with no hesitation, I grabbed the serrated knife from it's cozy little spot in the top drawer beside the stove. The kitchen lights above the stove reflected off of the knife. This drew my attention to my own reflection and I got a glimpse of the broken girl holding the knife. She was begging for help. Begging for the pain to stop.

Put the knife down and walk away, please. Just breathe. Everything will be okay. This isn't the answer. Cutting yourself will fix nothing.

It may not fix anything, but it will take away the pain. It may not be for long, but I'll get some fucking relief. This is who I am now; I can't help it, I just need to cut.

Please stop, this is not you, this is the person he created. You have been through enough pain and it is now time to heal. Put the knife down now! Please! No more pain, please don't do this again.

I placed the knife on my wrist, next to the row of scars that had been making their way up my forearm.

If you do this, he wins. If you cut yourself right now, he gets the satisfaction and he wins. This is you begging him. He's standing over you, smirking, enjoying, and basking in your pain.

I apply a small amount of pressure.

Please! Don't do this! Put the knife down! Walk away and cry it out. Call someone, scream into a pillow, or punch the damn pillow, just do not hurt yourself anymore!

I took another deep breath in and closed my eyes. I stood in the dim kitchen, knife pressed against my wrist lightly for a few moments. The silence was broken by the sound of metal hitting the ceramic floor. My heart was pounding hard against my chest. My face felt hot to the touch and a single drop of sweat left my forehead, travelled down the middle of my face and to the tip of my nose. The droplet fell.

I have hurt for the last few years of my life. It's time to stop. It's time to heal. Just because he hurt me, doesn't mean that I need to continue hurting myself. Don't let him win. You are in control now. He can't hurt you anymore. You are safe, you are loved, you are beautiful, and you are fierce. You are strong and you will get through this.

I picked up the knife and put it back in the drawer. I walked back down to the living room to put on a TV show until Sharon came back. I sat on the couch, thinking about my life and my decisions. I thought about who I was as a person.

I am the girl who loves. When I love, I love hard and I love with everything that I have. I am the girl who has had her heart broken and crushed time and time again, but I am also the girl who allows her heart to be broken so often. I give chance after chance to those who don't deserve it. Knowing the outcome, I choose my heart over my brain, no matter how damaged and hurt my heart is, it is the one who always ends up winning. I want to see the good in all and I want to believe because I am the girl who believes and the girl who dreams. Because of this, I get taken advantage of often. I am the girl who gets walked on, the girl who gets the blame and the girl who is thought of last. Despite all of this, I am always there for others and help whoever I can. I am a lover, I am a fighter, I am a mother, I am a dreamer, I am a believer, and I live with hope. I am also human and that means I get hurt. I get broken down and I have a limit. I have had to rebuild myself so many times, while picking up the pieces that have been shattered and having to leave some of those pieces behind. Continuing to find new ones to replace those missing and lost pieces.

For so long I allowed words like disappointment, failure, cunt, bitch, and worthless define who I was. I was constantly building myself around these words and definitions. These words no longer weigh me down. I chose to use these words to help motivate me. These words were left behind the last time I had to rebuild myself. I am not quite done, not finished or whole. A work in progress, building myself everyday into the person I want to be, not just for myself, but for my children as well.

Welcome to the zero tolerance zone. Zero tolerance for bullying, manipulation, and abuse. Zero tolerance for allowing others to treat my children and I poorly and walk all over us. For those that don't know who I am or how I live my life and chose to believe the vicious lies you spread, that's fine. Because I am choosing my children, I am choosing positivity and moving forward. I am choosing myself because if I don't, who will?

I spent years being tormented, abused, and hurt. Years standing alone in battle, years that were taken, and years I will never get back. Life is too short and precious. I am done. I will not allow one more damn minute to be taken away from these children or myself.

I know who I am. I am Victoria. I am not who I once was. Most of those who knew me, no longer do. I am new. I have a long journey ahead and my real life is just beginning. I could choose to let my life experiences take me down and lead me down a dark path. A path that would destroy and smother any hope of salvation. A path that would erase my hopes and dreams, creating even darker thoughts and a life that would ultimately destroy my children and me. But I don't want that. God, I don't fucking want that. I will fight my dark thoughts until they grow tired and retreat for good. I will fight those dark thoughts until the day I fucking die. They no longer control me. You no longer control me.

I walked upstairs to check on the boys, all sleeping in their beds. The three boys that were my light, my hope, and the boys that held all the love that my heart could possibly give. Today was unexpected, it was humiliating and devastating, but I am choosing to continue fighting through it. It's not the end. I knew it wasn't going to be easy to get over, but I knew I could do it.

I heard the front door open. Sharon was back. She was carrying some grocery bags filled with treats and snacks for the night.

I walked down the stairs and into the kitchen, where Sharon had placed all of the bags. "I'll grab the paint and canvases to take into the living room and we can find something on Netflix to watch."

Sharon turned and smiled. "Sounds good, I'll bring down the snacks! You holding up alright?"

I returned the smile and shook my head up and down. "I'll be fine. I'm not going to let it get me down. I shed my tears and I just really want to move past it. I know it's not going to always be easy, but I don't want to sit around crying for days, you know?"

Sharon shifted the bags to her one hand, placed the other on my shoulder, and squeezed gently. "You are so freaking strong. I will always be here for you too, don't forget that."

I placed my hand on hers. "Thank you, I know you will be and I will be here for you, no matter what."

We both smiled again and headed downstairs.

"Fun night of snacks and movies while we paint. Let's not forget the wine! We must crack that bad boy open." It had been a little while since Sharon and I had a good night like this. We both always had the kids and were fairly busy, so I appreciated the time spent together and her being here, especially tonight.

I laughed and grabbed the bottle. "Wine would be perfect right about now!"

I reflected on the fact that the night could have gone so differently. I sat there with Sharon, paint all over our hands and the floor, and a movie playing in the background. The positive outcome of this night came down to the choices I made. My entire life I had been making a lot of bad decisions. Lately, I felt like I was on a roll, like I was finally making the right choices. I was going down a good path that ended with a bright and happy future. I could have easily given in to my urges and hid it when Sharon got back. I also could have just called the night off entirely. Sat alone at home to be consumed by your demons, but I didn't.

37.

The police stopped by in the morning after the kids had gone to school. Sharon had to go home and pick up her little ones from her Mom's, so it was just Jayce and I at home. It was difficult talking to the police officer about what you had done. It was even more difficult having to show him the picture and the profile, but I got through it, one breath at a time. I didn't know what the outcome would be and I did have concerns about what you would do once you found out that I had called the police. It didn't matter anymore. I was tired of constantly worrying about what the repercussions I would have to face from disobeying you. It didn't matter what you would do because I was tired of hiding and I was going to do what was right from here on out.

I felt confident and strong. I was finally in control. The police said that they would follow up in about two weeks and that they needed enough evidence and more information before they move forward with charges. I was fine with that because I wasn't expecting anything immediate to happen. As long as we were making progress and you wouldn't get away with this anymore, I was happy.

You didn't even bother calling the kids that night, the night after, or any other night, for that matter. All communication had ceased. I knew the police had yet to talk to you. I also knew you were trying to build a case against me and somehow you would use this against me, but again, I tried not to worry about it. I was going somewhere. I had a new path and direction in my life. Having no contact was definitely a relief and lifted much stress and anxiety not only for me, but for the kids as well.

38.

Weeks went by before I received a phone call from the police.

"Miss Harrison?"

"Yes."

"This is Constable Young. I was just calling you to inform you that your ex-spouse was arrested this morning on the charges we had discussed a few weeks ago. He has been in the station for about five hours and we will be releasing him shortly. I wanted to call and let you know that there is a no-contact order that has been put in place immediately. So, if he tries to contact you, you are to call us and let us know right away, also if he shows up at your home or place of work."

I was overwhelmed with so many emotions. "Thank you, Officer Young. I appreciate everything you have done."

"Not a problem, Miss Harrison. If you need anything else or have any trouble, please don't hesitate to call."

"Thank you very much, will do. Take care." I hung up the phone and sat for a moment, trying to process the information the officer just gave me. This was a good thing. It wasn't bad. I was sure you were going to be beyond furious, but it was all going to be fine. You now knew that I wasn't going to allow you to continue this abuse and that I was strong enough to stand up for myself.

I took a few slow and deep breaths in and out. All I could do was prepare myself for whatever you did next to retaliate because oh boy, I knew you would. Anytime I tried to stand up for myself and push back you always pushed back 10 times harder. I knew it was going to come, so I just had to prepare myself. Whatever it was, I could come back from it. I mean, how bad could it be? Compared to the abuse at home, you trying to use my children to hurt me, setting your friend up to rape me, posting nudes of me on the internet for all to see. Honestly, how bad could it possibly get from here? I figured I had hit the bottom and all there was left was to start trying to climb my way back to the top. So, whatever you did next, I figured I would be okay. Plus, there was a no-contact order. That gave me a little safety reassurance, knowing that any form of contact meant you would be arrested again. I am going to be okay and the kids are going to be okay. Everything will be okay.

39.

Weeks had gone by since you had been arrested. Five amazing weeks. I didn't hear a word from you. There were no more emails and no more gathering the kids for their nightly call, the call that always caused them stress and anxiety. There was no mention of your name. No thinking about you at all. The kids and I were enjoying our freedom. We had finally taken some day trips to visit some family. After years of not being able to talk to them or see them. We went to the zoo, the museum, and some indoor parks. We took full advantage of life and we were finally living. No more struggling, no more money troubles, and no more abuse. I even had some extra money to spend on books and super hero toys for the kids since you were not around to spend it on junk, electronics, alcohol, and drugs.

I think that my favorite trip was to the zoo with my Mom, sister, and the kids. Jayce was so excited to see all the animals with his cousin, aunt, and Nana. We all played in the water park and finished the day with some ice cream and a train ride. Of course, Nana had to spoil the grand babies in the gift shop with stuffies of the animals we had seen that day and some little trinkets. I think this day was the kids' favorite as well. Seeing the pure joy in their eyes and them smiling ear-to-ear, made me forget the struggles we endured and the stress that once was. I didn't want to think about what could go wrong or what was to come next. I finally just wanted to live in the moment, cherish each minute of every day, and watch these kids enjoying life. This was all I really needed. I didn't need a man. I didn't need a million dollars or the best of everything because these kids were the best of everything. They were my reason. Greyson, the oldest and toughest guy in the house. He was so intelligent, loving and caring. Bentley was the wise one. He was just as caring and loving as Greyson, but he had this wisdom to him that just intrigued me. Then there was Jayce. The brave and fearless one. This kid literally had no fear. He was wild and free spirited, just like I once was. There were so many qualities they all shared but there were also so many unique qualities that made them their own special person.

I genuinely thought that from here on out, things were going to be good. Things were looking up and we were all going to be okay. We got through the worst of it and now it was time for the mending and healing part. The time for us to discover what life was really all about and to live it to the fullest.

It's taken me seven years to take back control of my life and I will never allow you to hurt me again. Do you hear me? This is my life now, I control it, not you. You will not win.

40.

On the 6th week of being completely free from you, we had decided to stay home and skip a day of school to go to the mall. The kids needed a few new shirts and shorts and I thought we could just make a day of it. Have some lunch and get some ice cream and maybe let the kids pick out a toy and a book each. After the mall, I wanted to come home and make a nice meal, have a camp out in the living room, and watch some Superman. The kids had been wanting to watch the original series from the beginning. The day went as planned. The kids loved the bus ride to the mall and thought it was so exciting to play hooky for the day. We bussed by the school and Greyson and Bentley laughed and giggled. They kept snickering to each other that they should be at school, but they were at the mall and having fun.

When we got to the mall, we picked up some subs for lunch and grabbed frozen yogurt before heading to all the stores. The kids picked out two shirts and two shorts each from Old Navy and then we headed to Coles, which was the kids' favourite book store. Each of them picked out a book and a Lego character from the front desk. When we finally got home with all our goodies, we washed up for dinner. I put on a roast with some potatoes and carrots while they played with their new Lego guys and read their books to each other.

After dinner we continued with our nightly routine: bath, teeth and pajamas. We took all our pillows and blankets down to the living room and set them up near the couch. We all cuddled up and watched Superman. Only Greyson made it to the end of the movie. Bentley and Jayce had fallen asleep about 45 minutes into the movie. They fought so hard to stay awake, but their sleepy little eyes just kept closing until they didn't open again and little snores hummed through the living room. Greyson fell asleep five minutes after the credits had finished. They all slept soundly. I decided to get up and clean up the dishes and rest of the house, now that they were out.

I cleaned the kitchen first and then made my way up the stairs to the rooms. I cleaned up any stray toys laying around and put the dirty laundry in the basket outside of the bathroom. When I was done cleaning, I ran the bath. I sat and soaked in the hot water for 15 minutes.

When I left the bath, I turned to go back downstairs to watch a little more TV before calling it a night. When I turned to face the stairs going down to the kitchen, I saw nothing but darkness. There was immense pressure and numbness on my face, especially my nose. After a moment, the numbness faded away. It felt as if I had a runny nose accompanied by a tingling sensation. I opened my eyes and could barely see. I saw black spots with a blurred background. I saw a figure come towards me and lean over my body. It was at this moment, I realized I was laying on the floor. I attempted to move my leg while reaching my arms out and trying to grasp the wall or anything close to me to help me stand up, but when I tried to move my foot, there was a sharp pain that shot up my entire leg. My vision was coming back, the blurriness fading slowly. I could now see. My ankle was broken and to my left, there you stood. You were staring deep into my soul with murderous rage. I knew you weren't leaving until you finished what you came here for.

In desperation, I began to drag my painful body to the kitchen. If I could somehow get to the kitchen, I could grab something to defend myself with. After making it about two feet into the kitchen, I heard three foot steps before feeling my broken ankle being crushed into the floor. The sound of my bone cracking rang in my ears. Before I could scream, your hand was squeezing my mouth shut. Your foot continued to twist and turn with force onto my ankle. Through muffled screams you smiled. I waved my hands and cried for you to stop. With your hand still covering my mouth, you could barely hear a word I was saying, but you knew. I continued to beg you to stop. It seemed that the more I begged, the bigger your smile became. A hand was then placed aggressively around my neck. Immediate pressure cut off my airway and nails dug deep into my skin, drawing blood. I could barely breath as I tried to frantically pry your hands off my neck. Not a word escaped your mouth. You removed your one hand from my mouth and choking echoed throughout the kitchen and hallway. Tears began to pool inside my ears, muffling the sound of my own choking. I tried to fight. I tried with everything I had, but it didn't matter. I knew this was the end.

Suddenly, I felt a sweet relief as you pulled your hands away from my neck. I gasped for air. Why did you let me go? I felt your arms lift my shoulders. You sat behind me, resting the back of my head against your chest. You hugged me for a brief moment and lifted my arm up.

"Ple- please. Don't." It hurt to speak. I felt that familiar burning and tearing sensation on my skin. I looked up to the blood pouring from my wrist. It trickled down my arm, dripping onto the floor. It was more than I had ever seen. You rubbed my hair with the hand you held the blade in. This really was it. There was no way out.

I thought about my boys and about how much I loved them. How much I wished I could be there to watch them grow and become men. Panic set in as I thought about who was going to take care of them now. Who would protect them and keep them safe? I tried one last attempt at breaking free of your grip, but I felt so weak and cold. My arm had gone limp as you held it above my head, holding the rest of my body with your other arm, preventing me from moving. Your arm wrapped tightly about my body, fist closed still holding the knife which now sat on my chest. I closed my eyes.

Why couldn't I have said goodbye just one last time? Darkness began to wipe away all memories, all thoughts, and feelings. I wasn't in pain anymore and I wasn't afraid. My breath slowed as the rest of my body became limp and lifeless. The only feeling I had left was the warm blood covering my cold body. I could feel the flow slowing down. I could feel my heartbeat fading. I took a deep breath in and saw one last little bit of my boys, laying in bed with me, laughing and jumping all over each other. The memory became more and more distant until I could no longer see it. I could just hear the faint laughter of Greyson, Bentley, and Jayce. Then there was darkness.

Epilogue.

A white chair sat in the middle of a small and dark room. A little barred window in the upper right corner of the room offered a glimpse of the moon light. The chair creaked as the man occupying it rocked back and forth. His left arm twitched, but only slightly as his arms were bound by a straightjacket. The buzz of the nurses station can be heard outside the door of this room. The man did not often have visitors and faced long days alone in this same position. The years were not kind to him. His once dark and tidy hair was now peppered with grey and thinning. He often screamed out in the night, "Victoria, Victoria, Victoria," but he refused any type of sedation because when he slept, she returned.

He fell asleep, sitting up, out of pure exhaustion. He was jolted awake by the transparent silhouette of a woman walking towards him. The woman was pale, wearing torn jeans with a blood stained t-shirt. As she came closer, out of the shadows and into the moonlight, you could see that her arms and hands were also covered in blood. A trail of drops followed behind. When she reached the man in the chair, she stopped and placed her hand on his shoulder. The man continued to look forward knowing that he was going to live his own nightmare for the rest of his life.

The woman bent down close to his ear and started to speak. "I was trapped and your demons had become my own......."

Resources.

National Domestic Violence Hotline

Toll Free: 1 (800) 799 – 7233
Available 24 hours a day, 7 days a week via phone and online chat.

The National Domestic Violence Hotline (The Hotline) is available for anyone experiencing domestic violence, seeking resources or information, or questioning unhealthy aspects of their relationship.

Love is Respect – National Teen Dating Abuse Hotline

Toll Free: 1 (866) 331 – 9474
Text: 22522
Available 24 hours a day, 7 days a week via phone, text, and online chat.

Love is Respect offers information, support, and advocacy to young people who have questions or concerns about their dating relationships.

National Suicide Prevention Lifeline

Toll Free: 1 (800) 723 – 8255
Available 24 hours a day, 7 days a week via phone and online chat.

The National Suicide Prevention Lifeline provides free and confidential support for people in distress, prevention and crisis resources for you and your loved ones, and best practices for professionals.

www.ingramcontent.com/pod-product-compliance
Lightning Source LLC
Chambersburg PA
CBHW031340060726
47590CB00007B/2553